RETURN TO SENDER . . .

"Death by Elvis," I murmured. "All around the big Elvis weekend. Sam, I have to call the cops." I dug around in my pocketbook for my cell phone. Unfortunately, when I tried to get a dial tone, it crackled static in my ear.

"Maybe if I go around to the side of the house, I can get a better signal."

"You can try," Sam said. "I'm getting out of here, personally." So saying, he turned to mist and fog.

"Terrific," I snapped. "When I really need you, you always seem to find somewhere else to be!"

I moved all the way down to the water. There I was rewarded with a clear dial tone. I was just punching in Officer Friendly's cell-phone number, when something grabbed me from behind.

I felt someone's hands on my shoulders, pulling me backward. Someone strong; their fingers hurt when they dug into me, right through my coat, and they were propelling me backward a lot faster than I wanted to go.

I hate surprises.

Previous books
in the Hollis Ball/Sam Wescott series

SLOW DANCING WITH THE ANGEL OF DEATH

DEAD DUCK

GHOST OF A CHANCE

GIVING UP THE GHOST

HELEN CHAPPELL

A DELL BOOK

Published by
Dell Publishing
a division of
Random House, Inc.
1540 Broadway
New York, New York 10036

The trademark Dell® is registered in the U.S. Patent and Trademark Office.

ISBN: 0-7394-0242-0

Printed in the United States of America

Dedicated to Elvis fans everywhere

GIVING UP THE GHOST

1

A FOOL SUCH AS I

♪ ♪ *"HI. THIS IS HOLLIS BALL, CRIME BEAT, Watertown* Gazette. *I'm on deadline or not at my desk right now, but if you leave a message, together with the time and date of your call, I'll get back to you as soon as I return to the news-room. Please wait for the beep before you start to speak. Thanks."*

Beep.

"Hi, Holly, honey. This is your long-lost godfather calling. I just got in from Vegas." (Silence.) *"Your godfather, Albie Lydekker? The Godfather of Odds?"* (Silence.) *"Look, I'm really sorry about the last time I was in town. I didn't know the gun was loaded, or was it the girl was married? Heh, heh, heh. And that*

thing about the screen door and, uh, the cows too. Um, I've got something going down to Toby's Bar right now. I mean, I'm having lunch here. Yeah, lunch. Can you call me here? Thanks. Oh, it's about eleven o'clock on Tuesday. Bye, now.''

Beep.

''Uh, Holly, this is, uh, Albie again. Seems like Toby's havin' a, um, little problem with my card game—I mean, bar bill. I offered him three-to-one odds, but he still wants cash. You couldn't come down here and lend me a half a yard, could you?'' (Unintelligible.) *''Okay, well, I'll try to get a hold o' Perk and Doll or Robbie or somebody and—who you callin' a washed-up ballplayer, you ass—''*

Beep.

''Goddamn it, Holly, where are you? It's Albie again, and I need—help! Don't do that, you—'' (Unintelligible.)

Beep.

Beep.

''Howdy, Hollis. This is Sheriff Bry Ackerman, over to the detention center? Listen, gal, we've got Albie Lydekker again. He got in some trouble down to Toby's, and we've got him up here on gambling without a license, drunk and disorderly, and resisting. He

says you'll bond him out, but I don't know if you want to or not, after the last time. I called Mr. Perk and he said to leave 'im here, which I can't say I blame 'im for. But if you want to bond 'im out, you can tell Big Tuna. Albie'll be up before the commissioner about eight, before the DWI's. Okay? Check ya later."

Beep.

Beep.

"Hey, Holly, Toby here. It's Wednesday morning. Tell that son of a bitch if he ever sets foot in my bar again, I'll kill him. Don't bail him out this time neither. He's got some scam about Elvis or somethin'."

Beep.

"Say, Hollis, it's Big Tuna, the bail bondsman? I called my wife and told her to make those plane reservations for Hawaii, 'cause Albie's back in town, heh heh. Two hundred fifty bucks is what I need if you want 'im out. He tried to roll craps for the bond, but not with his dice, heh, heh, I sez, heh heh heh." (Silence.) *"I wouldn't blame you if you let 'im stay there, after the last time he was in town. You know where to get me. Later."*

Beep.

Beep.

"Hollis, this is Judge Frank Carroll. I just heard Albie Lydekker's back in town. Can I see you in my chambers at noon? Thanks."

Beep.

(Heavy breathing.) Click.

Beep.

"Help! Holly! It's—" (Unintelligible.) Click.

Beep.

"Hollis, this is Terri over at the bank? Did you just write a two-hundred-fifty-dollar check to an Earl Scroggins's Bail Bonds? I just wanted you to know that your overdraft protection is going to be overextended, and I need to know if you want me to transfer funds from savings to checking to cover it. By the way, I heard Albie Lydekker's back in town." (Pause.) *"I'm so sorry."*

Beep.

"Hi, Holly. It's Albie. I must have gotten away from you back there at court somehow, since I've been banned from Toby's. I'm over to the Horny Mallard right now, and I'll have that two-fifty back to you as soon as I can find a card game, but first I need you

to do me a favor. Will you be a judge in the Chesapeake Chapter 'I Am Elvis' Interpreter Contest? I'm organizing it, see, it's a real job this time, I swear. . . . Trust me. Oh, it's gonna be an event to die for, not like the last time, you just wait and see!'' (Pause.) *''What can go wrong?''*

Beep.

2

VIVA LAS VEGAS

♪♪ I HAVE NO IDEA WHAT MY PARENTS WERE thinking when they asked Albie Lydekker to be my godfather. Of course, thirty-six years ago Albie was on his way up. He'd just been sent up to the Baltimore Orioles after a promising career in the triple A's, and it looked like the world was his oyster.

On the Eastern Shore of Maryland, where baseball is second only to Methodism as the state religion, Albie must have looked like a good deal at the time. He's my father's cousin, and the Lydekkers have been on Beddoe's Island since the first one fell off a Baltimore dredge boat and washed up on the bay shore a hundred years ago. And as my mother, Miss Doll, says, "*Most* of the Lydekkers are very nice people."

I guess they figured they'd made a mistake almost right away, because my brother told me that Albie showed up drunk at my christening and dropped me into the baptismal font. Headfirst, Robbie says, which accounts for me being the way I am. I think he's just jealous, since *his* godfather is a pillar of the V.F.D. and the church and a very dull and respectable gentleman indeed, but then again, so is Robbie.

One thing about having Albie as my godfather is that it has never been dull. He lasted a season with the O's before the wine, women, and betting on professional sports teams got him banned from baseball forever, or at least that's his story.

Boog Powell, who played with him for the O's, once told me that Albie's stats off the field were quite impressive, but a man with a hangover and a thousand dollars riding on the Colts makes a lousy pitcher.

Mr. Powell finally, reluctantly, told me that the *real* reason Albie was bounced from Major League Baseball was that he—Albie—had told Branch Rickey to kiss his ass. I guess the sheer intoxication of being at the show went to his head.

Sometimes, when you're a reporter, you don't know when to stop digging for answers, but for an iconoclast like me, something like that just burnished Albie's image as a rebel who lives by his own rules.

Alas, ever since my godfather was banned, it's been a slippery slope. For a few years he was a greeter at the Silver Spangle, a strip club over to the

Block in Baltimore. Last time I'd seen him, at our cousin Boink Ball's wedding, he'd borrowed a hundred dollars from me to put on a horse at Pimlico. The horse never made it over the finish line and I never saw that hard-earned hundred again, but I did get a lovely postcard of Death Valley, because something happened in Baltimore around that time and Albie suddenly found pressing business in Las Vegas.

And evidently, pressing business had kept him there for several years of complete and total silence. Which I could understand: At Boink's wedding reception over to the Oysterback fire hall, there was some business with Albie, Junior Redmond, and Hudson Swann about a stolen cow, a '63 pink Cadillac, a hole in the Oysterback post office door, and some alleged beings from the planet Uranus who weren't. After that incident it seemed like a good idea for Albie not to come around the Eastern Shore for a long time. So I guess Vegas looked like a good option.

Even though I have few if any illusions left about Albie, I love him and was thrilled to know he was back in town. When I was growing up, Albie's erratic and infrequent appearances in my life were always like a surprise birthday–Christmas all rolled into one. No matter how his life was going, Albie always had a present for me and an unshakable belief in my ability to become a writer. A belief that was shared by no one else, including my English teachers.

It was Albie who bought me my first typewriter, a

tiny Olivetti manual, and Albie whose great glamour as a sort-of-famous ballplayer gave me what little social cachet I had in high school.

As a girl growing up down on the island, Albie Lydekker represented a larger, more glamorous world outside the provincial Eastern Shore. A world that I thought beckoned to me, until I got out there into it and found out what real life is really like. So in a way I owe Albie, but I still have to take him with a large chunk of salt.

Even knowing all that, when I met Albie at the Horny Mallard Pub that afternoon after posting his bond, some of that old starry magic was still there. And I was ready for some magic.

After the holidays are over and the Christmas lights have been taken down, January looms ahead of us like a big dead white hole, a month to be crawled through like a long tunnel. A tunnel that will open into spring, but not until you suffer through the winter. Albie's sudden appearance was just what I needed to lose my post-holiday blues and slog through one of the longest, most bitter cold spells we'd had in a long time.

But even I could sense that Albie's latest get-rich-quick scheme had a series of holes so large you could have driven a Volkswagen through them.

"The Chesapeake Chapter of the Elvis Tribute Artist Society?" I heard myself repeating. I looked at the story below the fold on the front page of today's *Gazette,* hot off the presses. Since I'd booked out of the newsroom to rescue Albie as soon as I went off deadline, this was all news to me.

ELVIS CONTEST TO COME TO WATERTOWN
Local Impersonators to Pay Tribute to King

Jolene, the *Gazette*'s community editor, had her byline on it, so of course I had to read it three times before I understood the gist of the story. I was still puzzling through lines like *Shore King tribute artists will personally impersonate Elvis in order to pay tribute to the King, who is much beloved among local Elvis fans at the Waterside Theater who remember local native Albie Lydekker as a famous Baltimore Oriole Bird of the mid-sixties who is in charge of the contest. . . .*

The fact that the lovely and talented Jolene is office snitch and *maîtresse-en-titre* to Rig Riggle, the *Gazette*'s editor from hell, gives her more job security than the rest of us hardworking newsroom rats, many of whom can write a story you can actually read. My lips moved and a slight headache began to form as I plowed through Jolene's tormented syntax. My own name leapt out of the newsprint at me like a trap-door spider. "Wait a minute!" I barked. "Albie, what's this mean? *'Among the prominent local judges selected to select the Chesapeake Elvis Tribute Artist will be Hollis Ball, award-winning* Gazette *reporter and Judge Frank Carroll, Circuit Court for Santimoke*

County'—Albie, what the pluperfect hell—'' I howled.

"I knew you wouldn't mind! It can't miss, Holly!" Albie promised me as he gobbled down his cheese steak. "I'm on my way back up again! I'll even cut you in on a piece of the action!"

If I had a nickel for every time Albie has blown into town and told me he was on his way back up, I could quit my crummy reporter job and lie on the couch all day reading cheap novels, eating Reese's Peanut Butter Cups, and watching old movies on AMC. That I am still slogging the cops-and-courts beat for the Watertown *Gazette* (motto: *Thou Shalt Not Offend the Advertisers*) says a lot about Albie's luck.

"You could have at least asked me first! And Frank! Albie, you *know* Frank isn't going to go for the foolishness of looking at a lot of watermen in cheap spangled jumpsuits and bad black wigs! He's a dignified man, for God's sake! He's a sitting judge! We just finished a high-profile, capital homicide trial last night, and I'll make a bet that he's in a mood this morning! He's going to nail your ass to the wall when he sees this!''

Albie perked up considerably when he heard the word *bet,* but I don't think anything else I said even penetrated. I studied him. The years had not been kind to my godfather. He was easily on the long side of fifty, and his red hair looked as if it came from a bottle these days, but he was still as tall and gangly as the heron, to whom he bore a remarkable likeness. He must have been nearly six-five and weighed about one fifty-five, a carrot-haired scarecrow of a man.

I watched as Donna, the bartender, added some figures to my tab. Albie, as usual, was dead broke. After yesterday's altercation at Toby's and his night in the tank, there was reddish-gray stubble on his jaw, and his plaid sports coat and aqua silk shirt didn't look quite as snappy as they might have, but he still sported his Rolex watch and his hideous ruby ring, which he considered his good-luck charms. Like a lot of ballplayers, Albie is incredibly superstitious.

"This is the deal. When I got back from my, uh, stay in Vegas, I, uh, ran into Vera and Lucca Devine, who, uh, saw my potential and got me on the ground floor of the Elvis Impressionist Society. It's got to be legit, Holly, it's incorporated in Delaware!"

Albie blinked at me. "Lucca 'Bang Bang' Devine, the capo of the Devines?" I asked. The Devines, a very minor crime family, used to own the action in the Baltimore–Washington corridor until Carlo "The Crab" Devine was found floating in Inner Harbor attached to the transmission of an '89 Cavalier. As far as crime families went, the Devines were where the gene pool met the cement pond. My friends on the Baltimore *Sun* tell me it's the crack crews you want to worry about now.

Baltimore and Washington, just across Chesapeake

Bay, are Sodom and Gomorrah to a true Eastern Shore person, which is what I am.

"Aw, that was just some ugly rumors," Albie said dismissively as he shoved some cottage fries into his mouth. "Bang Bang's in the entertainment industry now. Completely legit."

"Let me see if I have this straight," I said carefully. "You are gainfully employed by Bang Bang Devine to set up and organize an Elvis impersonator contest on the Eastern Shore. Then the winner goes to the Maryland finals, and the winner of that goes to the national contest, in Vegas."

"That's right." Albie grinned. "Viva Las Vegas!"

"And these Baltimore sleazes—I mean, people—sent you to organize it," I mused. "An Elvis impersonator contest."

"We call them interpreters. Elvis interpreters, or Elvis tribute artists," Albie replied with vast dignity. He leaned toward me. "Listen, Elvis is like a religion to a lot of people. I mean, he's the King. The fine folks who pay tribute to him by impersonating—I mean, interpreting—the King are doing the world a favor!"

"Elvis? The God of Excess?" I asked nastily. "The man who furnished a whole house in wall-to-wall gold-lamé leopard-print shag rug and OD'd on the toilet?"

"And I want you to be one of the judges," Albie

said, just as if he hadn't heard me, which was so typical of him.

"Oh, I don't think so!" I replied. "Albie, I don't volunteer for anything! Besides, I know nothing about Elvis. Or I know enough to know I don't want to know any more—"

"This is a sure thing, Holly. We're going to hold the contest at the old cocktail lounge at the Lock and Load Motor Inn. I know, I know, the lounge has been closed down for years, since they lost their liquor license, but we're gonna fix it up with a coat a paint, and the tribute artists are going to rehearse there! It'll be a class production, I promise. There'll be about fifty interpreters competing! It's gonna draw a huge crowd, you wait and see! And the great thing is, first prize is a pair of blue suede shoes worn by the King himself!"

Stars glittered in Albie's eyes. When I saw that his gaze was directed at Donna's lissome behind, I sighed. Albie loves women, and for some reason they love him right back. The problem is that Albie always ends up in trouble himself, because the women he attracts always seem to have a boyfriend or a husband or a large masculine girlfriend in the background they forgot to mention.

"Oh, it's gonna be great! The Night of the Elvii!" Albie continued.

"Elvii?"

"Plural Elvis, honey. Anyway, I know you'll want to come on board!"

"What about Frank Carroll? Frank swore if he ever saw you again he'd direct to indict after that incident with the fake Martian landing—"

"Uranians. Uranians!" Albie swept that incident away with a wave of his hand. "Don't worry about Frank! Frankie Carroll and I used to play ball together back on the old Delmarva Farmers! We was literally a farm team, you bet!"

"Oh, my God." I sighed. As I was reaching for a handful of boiled peanuts, I watched Donna taping a big blue and silver poster to the back bar mirror. BE ELVIS, it said above a big picture of the King in full Vegas drag with a blue and silver full body halo emanating from his glittering body. PROCEEDS TO EASTERN SHORE CHILDREN'S CANCER FUND, it said along the bottom, but it was almost lost in the splashy aura radiating from a canonized King.

"It's gonna be great, I promise! Look, the Devines said if I do this right, they'll sign me on permanently! I could be like Bert Parks! This is gonna be bigger than Miss America!"

"I dunno. I don't think I want to see an Elvis swimsuit contest," I muttered dubiously.

Albie patted my hand. "Come on, Holly. What can go wrong?" He leaned over and grinned at me. "Besides, I'm into Bang Bang for ten big ones, and he says he'll cancel the debt if I can do this."

"Ten big what?" I yelped. "Albie, what've you done now?"

"So, I had a run of bad luck at blackjack." Albie shrugged. "It's not like he's gonna break my legs or anything. At least, I don't think so." He grinned at me sheepishly.

"Holl! Beware!" a voice cried in my ear. I looked around and saw no one there. A tingly little feeling, like small, cold fingers tapping on the back of my neck, warned me of what was coming, so I wasn't too terribly surprised when the ghost of Sam Wescott, my late and ex-husband, appeared on the barstool behind Albie's.

Oh, great. Just what I needed, I thought.

"Who let him in?" Sam asked, glowering at Albie. But, of course, only I heard, and I was trying to ignore him.

Sam haunts me, but it's a long story. Of course, only a few others can see or hear him, which makes it even more interesting. For him anyway. For me he's a general pest who seems to appear in my life at the least opportune moments.

"Don't do it," Sam pleaded, glowing like a nuclear reactor in his angst. "Please, Hollis, don't do this. You know what Albie's like!"

I gave Sam a dirty look, then smiled weakly at my hapless godfather. "The idea of some mob guy breaking your legs is too much for me to handle," I sighed.

"I'd like to break his legs," Sam growled, staring

furiously at the back of Albie's head. "Someone from the island would do it for a case of beer; why go to foreigners for the same service?" he muttered. He leaned over and sort of inhaled at Albie's drink, which is how a ghost gloms up food and drink. They suck up the essence of it. So next time something tastes flat, consider that a ghost may have gotten there first.

"Sign me up," I beamed with a nasty look at my own personal ghost.

"Oh, shit." Sam put his translucent head in his translucent arms. "Here we go again."

"Shut up, Jiminy Cricket," I hissed at Sam, who shook his head and discorporated, leaving behind a nasty smile that hung in the smoky bar air for just a second.

"Huh?" Albie said, looking behind him. But, of course, he saw nothing.

"I said, 'Oh, Jiminy Cricket! What fun this will be!'" It sounded weak, even to me, but sometimes Sam provokes me so much I have to say *something* to him, even though it makes me look nuts. More nuts, some people would say.

He took a sip of his drink and frowned. "This tastes like the ginger ale went flat all of a sudden," he complained. But Albie was oblivious. He was already eyeing something on the counter. "Look, Hollis, see those two droplets of water running down the bar top?

I'll bet you the tab that the one on the right hits my glass before the one on the left.''

"I don't take sucker bets, Albie," I cut in quickly. "Look, about this Elvis thing—"

Across the street, the courthouse clock chimed twelve times. "Frank!" I exclaimed, looking at my watch. "This is why he wanted me to meet him in his chambers at noon!" Hastily, I began to gather up my stuff. "This is all your fault, Albie. If Frank kills me I'm holding you responsible."

"You're meeting up with Frank right now?" I could see the lights going off in his head. Maybe it was just misfiring synapses, I hoped.

"None better," I muttered, grabbing up a handful of Goldfish crackers. It wouldn't be my first bar lunch or my last.

"Well, I'll just mosey on across the street with you," Albie said. "Then we'll get this settled up right away. I got a whole lotta publicity to do today, places to go, people to see!"

"Albie, after that incident with the cows, the screen door, and those Ukrainians at Boink's wedding, I don't think you should pull Frank's chain too hard—"

"Uranians. They was from the planet Uranus. Aw, Frank's a good ole boy." Albie brushed away my concerns with one hand. "Le's go talk to him."

I wished I'd remembered to pack my Kevlar vest this morning. I had a feeling I was going to need it.

3

MEMORIES

"LYDEKKER, YOU LOW-RENT, SCUM-sucking, bottom-feeding son of a bitch!"

His Honor, Judge Franklin Carroll of the Circuit Court of the State of Maryland, yelled, waving the morning edition of the *Gazette* in my godfather's face. "I don't want to hear my name on your lips!"

Now, you have to understand that Frank Carroll is a lawyer, so he chooses his words pretty carefully, but I really didn't like the way he was looking at Albie, like he was a child molester or worse.

"Carroll, you low-life pond sucker!" Albie replied happily, and the two of them punched each other's arms like butthole buddies.

My mouth was probably hanging open, but those two were so happy to see each other that I was forgotten. I'd expected that Frank would be in a mood, but I hadn't anticipated it would be a good one.

With his black robes flapping all around him, Frank looked like a happy minister. He was not a tall man, and his thick crown of platinum-silver hair sprung up all over his head, as it does when he pushes his hands through it during long sessions on the bench. Beneath his thick white eyebrows, his blue eyes sparkled.

"You miserable son of a bitch, where the hell have you been?" the judge demanded. He opened the bottom drawer of his desk and brought out the bottle of Wild Turkey he keeps there for emergencies. When you run a circuit court on the Eastern Shore in the great state of Maryland, an emergency can be anything from a jury returning a death penalty to a divorcing spouse having a fainting fit. Frank says the only happy people he ever sees are the adoptive families. For them, he keeps helium balloons in the closet.

Clearly, Albie was more of a Wild Turkey than a balloon event. Frank even sprung for some clean paper cups from the bathroom.

"I'm off for the rest of the day," he said, pouring us each a judicious finger of amber liquid. "Just don't let my clerk catch us at this." He winked. "We finished up a five day last night. All I've got now is the usual stack of paperwork."

"I'm off deadline," I said. Neither of us bothered to ask what Albie had planned. The idea of him actually working was too much like science fiction.

My judicial mentor sank into the chair, behind his desk and savored his drink. "Ahhh." He sighed. "What a morning. I just had a capital sentence go to appeals, and all hell's broken loose. Shaw, the weed-whacker murderer."

"This is about a thousand times better than the swill we used to get from Babe Willis's still down below when we was with the Delmarva Farmers."

"Now, that was some bad 'shine." Frank sighed as he leaned back in his chair, ignoring the piles of folders that had a better claim to his attention than we did. He had another sip of bourbon. "Do you remember when we used to go down below Cambridge? We'd play against the Vienna All-Stars, then we'd go fishing all night—both teams—then we'd play ball again the next day. . . ."

The memories were rolling. I was content to sit and become invisible, as a good reporter should be, while the pair of them reviewed old times, probably through a rosy haze, definitely with nostalgia.

I sat and half-listened to tales of a time when Frank and Albie were young, and life was before them, and they were semipro ballplayers—hot studs, to hear them tell it. I was relieved that Frank had forgotten why I had been summoned and that he wasn't going to kill Albie, that I was home free and could sneak out eventually.

Frank dropped the *Gazette* on his desk, and I glanced at the front page. I really should start reading the paper I work for, no matter how painful it can be to see my copy edited with an ax. The Wild Turkey slid smoothly down my throat and blurred the edges just a little.

Fully occupied covering the trial, I'd been paying little attention to what was happening around the county.

But Albie and Frank were rambling on down memory lane. ''There we were in a broken-down bus in a pouring rainstorm in the middle of East Jesus, somewhere up-shore, with a broken-down bus and a driver so drunk he couldn't find his ass with two hands and a road map, and Belcher ate that bad barbecue and was throwing up all over the back of the bus—''

''Those two girls in Elkton who—''

''. . . crawling over the fence to sneak out of that ballpark before they could . . .''

Those two were lost in the past somewhere back in the fifties. My eye fell on a small piece down in the corner of the page, well below the fold. It was only a couple of inches long, but the headline caught my attention.

COUNCIL HEARS PROPOSAL FOR GAMBLING CASINO

I scanned it quickly. At their last meeting the Santimoke County Council had listened to a presentation
by B and B Enterprises of Baltimore outlining the
benefits of establishing a gambling casino here: more
jobs, more tourists, more money, yada yada. The
council had made no comment and had tabled discussion on the matter until a later date. They had taken
under consideration the opportunity to visit another B
and B casino in the Midwest—all expenses paid by B
and B. Yada yada.

Gambling, I yawned. It could never happen here.

But, of course, it did. Fire departments regularly
offered games of chance at their fund-raisers.
Churches held car or quilt raffles; private clubs like
the Elks and the Moose had slot machines where the
money went to local charities. Even the library offered a basket of cheer, and God knows, Maryland
had a state lottery into which I sometimes lost a dollar
or two in a vain hope of hitting the number. It had
been my understanding that Lotto had been designed
to enrich public education; when it started going into
welfare for a billionaire, building a huge new stadium
for his football team, I stopped playing. But I personally have been known to play cards for money, if you
count a quarter and dime pot as money. But a casino?
All those glittering lights and cocktail waitresses and
seminude muscle boys were too tacky for redbrick
colonial Santimoke County, where Hysterical Preser-
vation is a way of life.

My reporter sense was tingling again, and again I ignored it. I know what you are thinking, and you are probably right.

"Do you remember those young guys who stopped their car to help us? That hillbilly band?" Albie was asking, and the laughter of the two middle-aged men sucked me back into the present.

"Who knew?" Frank shook his head. "Who in hell knew?"

"That kid with the greasy hair—"

"And there we were in Galena one Sunday night, and someone turned on the TV, and there he was, on *Ed Sullivan,* by damn! That same boy who got our bus started down there in Mount Vernon that night!"

"Elvis Presley was a good mechanic; no one ever gives him any credit for that," Albie intoned mournfully. "He majored in shop in high school."

"He got that old bus running, didn't he?" Frank sighed.

"I woulda liked to take him gunnin'. He woulda liked that. It's a lot more fun shootin' geese than TV's."

"Poor son of a bitch." Frank sighed. "The way he ended up, it was just tragic."

"You guys met Elvis Presley?" I snapped back into the moment.

My godfather and my mentor turned to look at me as if they'd forgotten me. I could see why they were irritated. Back there in the fifties Albie and Frank were young and irresponsible and handsome. In the present they were a couple of guys on the downhill of 50, with receding hairlines and eroding prostates.

"Well, yeah." Albie blinked. "We met him, yeah."

"Get outta here! You guys?"

"Why not us guys?" Frank asked, hurt. "You think we were never hep? You kids think you invented rock and roll?"

"Yeah," Albie intoned solemnly. "We was there from the beginning, you know."

"We rocked around the clock." Frank snapped his fingers, then winced at his arthritic knuckles.

"We were snappy in those days. You shoulda seen us in our uniforms. We had the chicks fallin' all over us."

"How come you never told me about meetin' Elvis before?" I asked suspiciously.

Albie blinked at me. "You never ast us," he said reasonably.

"Elvis Presley fixed your bus?" I persisted dubiously.

"He sure did," Frank declared. "The Delmarva Farmers' bus broke down in the mountains near Deep Lake after a game with the Cumberland Hornets. Three in the morning, in the middle of nowhere, and this truck pulled up with the wildest bunch of hillbilly musicians you ever saw. That was Elvis and his band, coming from a date at some club in Garret County.

He wasn't rich and famous yet, just a kid with greasy hair and a wild pink and black jacket. But he took a look at the bus engine and figured how to make it work. Loose wire or something.''

"It was Elvis, all right! Ask Orville Lovejoy or Poot Wallop or any of the old Farmers!'' Albie insisted. ''You coulda knocked us all over with the same feather when he showed up on *Ed Sullivan* a year or so later! That's why Frank's gonna be a judge in the Elvis contest! We've gotta history with the King!''

"Now, wait a minute, Albie, I never said—'' Frank protested, but Albie threw an arm around the judicial shoulders.

"C'mon, Frank, remember the old days? It'll be fun!'' Albie cajoled. ''We can have a few laughs about this one, just like we done back with the Farmers.'' He winked. ''Besides, I already put your name in the press release. You ain't gonna make a liar outta me, are you?''

"Well,'' Frank said uncertainly, but you knew that he was falling under Albie's spell, just like he used to when they were playing doubleheaders a long time ago.

"Frank, you are a pal!'' Albie said, slapping the judge on the back and splashing a little more of the man's own Wild Turkey into his Styrofoam cup.

"Maybe so.'' Frank sighed. ''But I'll tell you what—if I had any of those goddamned Elvis impersonators in my courtroom, I'd direct a guilty verdict!''

"Looks like someone beat you to it, Frank." Bailiff Bob Winters stood in the doorway, jingling the change in his pocket. "I just come up from over to the sheriff's office." He fluttered some papers at the judge. "Radio said they just found a guy dead at the Lock and Load Motor Inn out on Route 50. And Bry Ackerman said he looks just like Elvis."

4

HEARTBREAK
HOTEL

♪♪ THE CORPSE HAD A FAMILIAR FACE.
It was just hard to see it, the way it was
sprawled facedown on the grungy bathroom floor. But that blue-black pompadour sure did
look as if it belonged on you-know-who. And there
was no mistaking the flange-collared white jumpsuit,
spangled with glittery sunbursts and sequined half-
moons, pulled down around the flared and fringed
pants around his ankles, exposing an unprepossessing
full moon and a pair of white and hairy legs.

From where I was standing in the motel doorway, the body was doing a fine impression of Dead
Elvis.

"Looks like he died and fell off the terlet, Sarge,"
Corporal Harvey Baynard said to Detective Sergeant

Ormand Friendly, who was looking around the dingy room distastefully. The place was crammed with crime-scene types, photographing, dusting, looking into drawers and under the sagging bedframe. "Probably an overdose. But jeez, he sure looks like, you know, that Vegas guy."

It was so cold in the room that our breath clouded the air. I frowned. It was almost as cold inside as it was out. Maybe they didn't believe in heat at the Lock and Load. More likely it was the open bathroom window, letting in the chill air and giving a view of the empty fields behind the motel.

Friendly sighed and pulled at his Grateful Dead necktie, loosening it from his rumpled blue shirt. " 'That Vegas guy' was the King of Rock and Roll," he said absently, making notes in his little spiral-bound book.

"He don't *look* like Springsteen," Harve said. Freshly promoted to plainclothes, he looked about seventeen. When cops and teachers start to look absurdly young, you know you are getting o-l-d.

"That's the Boss," I said, taking a chance by lifting the yellow crime-scene tape and stepping into the motel room. "Elvis is the King." I nodded pleasantly at the videotaper, who was doing a sweep of the cheap furniture and the unmade bed. If you had to die somewhere, Room 13 of the Lock and Load Motor Inn was just about the saddest place you could pick.

NO COOKIN IN ROOM
NO IRONIN ON RUG
NO NOYSE AFTER TEN
THIS MEANS YOU!!!

read the hand-lettered sign on the wall by the door.

"Hollis! I should have known you'd be here. It's okay, Harve, she won't touch anything, she's with me," Friendly growled. "This place already looks like a carnival blew through here. Everyone and their mother went in and out of this room before anyone thought to call us," he added grimly, flipping his notebook shut. "One more snoop won't contaminate the scene any more than it already is!"

"Nice to see you too." I smiled.

Friendly glowered at me. "What the hell do you think we've got here?" he asked, gesturing toward the open bathroom door, where two paramedics were getting ready to scrape up the stiffened stiff, sequined white jumpsuit and all.

The next place this guy was gonna pay tribute to the King was the medical examiner's office in Baltimore. I turned away.

"Lenny Bruce having a real bad hair day?" I asked cheerfully. "A Judy Garland wannabe who went terribly, terribly wrong?"

"Very funny," Friendly snapped, but a couple of uniforms snickered. "It looks like an OD. We found a pile of pills on the nightstand. Percodan, Ativan,

Librium, Seconal, Quaalude, you name it. God only knows what else. A regular drugstore of downers." I cast a glance at the candy-colored capsules spilled across the scarred surface of the table. A tech was photographing it.

"Valsalva maneuver," I said. Friendly suddenly grinned, softening the hard lines in his face.

"I think you're learning something after all!" he said approvingly.

"Downers, especially morphine and synthetic morphine, can constipate you; they paralyze the sphincter muscles. You have a weak heart or hardened arteries, you strain very hard at stool, you can have a heart attack or apoplexy and die right there on the toilet," I recited. "Coronary or stroke brought on by accidental or deliberate overdose?"

Friendly nodded again. "I'll make a cop out of you yet. Or at least a good crime reporter. Of course, we won't know till the M.E. runs a tox scan, but it sure looks that way."

"Looks like the King died on his throne," one of the paramedics muttered, and they both laughed as they awkwardly turned the corpse onto his back. He was well into rigor mortis. His bony knees and bent elbows made shifting him onto the gurney awkward. Then they both gasped at once. "Uh-oh," one of them said.

From the front he didn't look so much like Elvis, but it was hard to tell. He was a purplish color, his eyes were popping out of his head, and his swollen tongue was thrust firmly into the rictus of his teeth.

"Say, Sarge," Harve said uncertainly, "this guy looks like an asphyxiation, not an OD."

Friendly swore softly as he bent to examine the dead man. "I'll be damned," he said, pulling back the flanged collar to reveal what looked like a red rope wrapped tightly around his neck. "How in hell did we miss this?"

"We just assumed, with all the pills . . ." Harve stammered.

"Never assume anything." Friendly sighed, pulling on a pair of latex gloves before gingerly unwinding the red rope. It had been wound so tightly around the dead man's neck that it had left a depression in the mottled flesh, and Friendly had some trouble loosening it. "Let's get some pictures here! Come on, move it!"

The photographer moved it, taking shots of the dead man from every angle.

Finally, as we all watched, Friendly slowly extracted a long, thin red scrap of fabric from the man's neck, holding it up for all of us to see. "A scarf," he announced. "Looks like the sumbitch was strangled with an Elvis scarf."

"A cheap Elvis scarf," I sneered. "That's not silk, it's polyester."

Friendly looked at me as if he was seeing me for the first time, and before he could tell me to get lost, I stepped back and allowed the professionals to take over. Anyway, I'd seen more than I wanted to see. The guy was not a pretty sight.

"Looks as if someone come up alongside of him while he was sitting there and got him good," Harve said.

Friendly grunted.

I stepped aside as they wheeled the remains out to the waiting ambulance. The corpse's stiffened arms and legs tented the urethane body bag like a grotesque sculpture.

We all watched him go.

"What I can't figure out is why he was wearin' that Elvis suit," Friendly muttered. He was carefully placing the red scarf into a plastic evidence bag.

"We recovered the deceased's wallet, Sarge." A uniformed cop walked into the room, holding a leather billfold between latex-coated fingers. "Seems like a woman down the corridor helped herself to it. She and him had a little party last night, she said. She came back this morning for more, saw that he was dead, and helped herself."

"That would be Snow White," I offered. "She's a—well, she lives here. As you may have noticed, the Lock and Load Motor Inn ain't exactly the Fuzzy Bunny Bed and Breakfast." I looked at the stained rug distastefully. "And yes, Snow White is her real name."

"Ah, the seamy side of lovely Santimoke

County." Friendly sighed as he took the proffered billfold. "The stuff the tourists don't see."

"This one evidently did," I pointed out. "Was he in town for the Elvis contest?"

"What Elvis contest?" Friendly riffled through the wallet and whistled as he pulled out a driver's license. He muttered a long string of expletives and did not repeat himself once. "Looks like we got trouble right here in River City," he rumbled, handing the wallet to Harve, who also whistled when he looked at the license.

"Okay, Hollis, hon, on outta here. You've seen all you're gonna see," Friendly said briskly, shooing me away.

"Hey! I've got my rights! The public has a right to know—" I reached for the license, but the man steered me toward the door. So much for conflict of interest. When things get interesting, my so-called boyfriend puts me out.

"That's all for now," he said firmly.

I was amazed I'd gotten as far as I had, actually. Cop cars and ambulances were not an uncommon sight at the Lock and Load. People rented rooms here, and when their government checks were used up on crack and smack and booze, they were evicted. Then they slept in their cars in the parking lot until the first of the month, when the whole cycle started up again.

The Lock and Load was a low, crumbling cinder-block building painted a fading and hideous pink. It

had seen better days and done better things, back in
the fifties, when it was new. Even the sunlight looked
shabby here, where the neon sign by the highway
buzzed like a nest of hornets and the smell of neglect
and fast food from the Dippy Donut next door hung
over everything like a fog. Weeds pushed their way up
between the widening cracks in the concrete, and the
parking lot was decorated with broken-up asphalt and
some brave pots of plastic geraniums. Down at the far
end of the building, the empty cocktail lounge didn't
look as if it was undergoing any major renovations.
The windows were boarded up, and the neon COCK-
TAILS sign hadn't blinked since 1977, when the liquor
board closed it down for serving minors. It had enjoyed a glamorous reputation in the fifties; now it just
looked sad and past its prime, like the old folks and
the transients who called it home.

If I owned the Lock and Load Motor Inn and hell,
I'd rent out the Lock and Load and live in hell. I was
convinced of that when I saw a familiar local character making his way toward us.

"What's goin' on here?" Elvis Man yelled.

Uh-oh.

The tiny man with an enormous pompadour of
greasy blond hair as tall as he was, wedged his way in
the door. "I'm Rolley Shallcross, the manager here!"
he was yelling. "I run a clean place here. I don't
tolerate troublemakers! What the hell is goin'—" He
stopped when he saw the corpse through the open

door of the meat wagon. His pink face drained of color, and he adjusted his thick aviator glasses. ''That's not Bang Bang, is it?'' he gasped. ''Oh, dear, oh, dear, oh, dear!'' The feistiness just drained out of him.

''That's Elvis Man!'' Harve muttered. ''I didn't know Elvis Man had a real name.''

''I thought his name *was* Elvis Man,'' I agreed. ''He *manages* this place?''

''Can I have a word with you, Mr., uh, Shallcross?'' Friendly asked, taking Elvis Man by the arm. Somewhere between thirty and death, he was so short that he came up only to my man's shoulder, but he made up for his lack of height with that astounding wave of hair. You needed shades just to look at his clothes too. He was wearing a brown and pink plaid sports jacket and one of those bolo ties that sported what looked like an enormous silver nugget—until you looked closely and saw that it was Elvis Presley's head. And yes, he was wearing blue suede shoes. And two diamond pinkie rings. He looked like he'd been caught in a fifties' time warp. He matched the decor of the Lock and Load.

''Hey, Elvis Man,'' Harve greeted him.

''Harve, what's goin' on here?'' Shallcross bleated.

''Talk to the man.'' Harve gestured toward Friendly.

''That can't be Bang Bang!'' Rolley Shallcross

fretted, torn between talking to the cops and watching the techs close the door on the body in the meat wagon.

I studied him closely. It would have been hard not to. He was a local celebrity. "That's Elvis Man," Harve told Friendly.

Elvis Man roamed around town, often in a glittery homemade jumpsuit, happily singing Presley tunes to himself. He was one of those harmless eccentrics who become part of the scenery in places like Watertown. Every place has one, and they're especially thick on the ground on the Shore, where we have characters we haven't used yet. Down on the island, it's Miss Erna, the Cat Lady, who lurks around the harbor leaving out cans of Whiskas for the strays.

"Well," I whispered to Harve as we watched Elvis Man talking nervously to Friendly, "it's nice to know he's gainfully employed."

"He's different," Harve noted. "He's not right, you know. He was a change-of-life baby."

"Oooh." I nodded. In Eastern Shore–ese I had just been informed that Elvis Man was probably a few IQ points around dull-normal and had some behavior problems that may have had to do with his mother's menopausal state at his birth.

"But he's harmless," Harve hastened to reassure me. "In fact, he gets along all right. His parents left him a house and some money, and Terri, over to the bank? She's his cousin, and she takes care of his bills and stuff, so he makes out okay. He just likes to sing like Elvis, that's all.''

"Yeah, I've seen him around in his little outfit.'' Our breath hung in the air in blue clouds.

"I didn't know he had a job though.'' Harve scratched his mustache. "Maybe that's why this place is such a mess,'' he added matter-of-factly. "I don't think Elvis Man has enough on the ball to look after something like this.''

"He sure is upset about this murder,'' I observed, watching the little man wipe away tears and wring his hands as he talked to Friendly, who obviously didn't have a clue as to Elvis Man's backstory. He looked frightened and confused, like a child who is lost in a department store.

"Probably he thinks it was the real Elvis who died. He innit right, you know.'' Harve sighed and hitched up his belt. "I'd better go straighten Sarge out. Sometimes, with people from away, they don't know how it is.''

"Especially with Friendly.'' We exchanged a look of understanding, and Harve made his way toward the two men.

"Well, I don't know anything!'' a sharp voice exclaimed. Off to one side, under the sagging portico, I saw a scrawny woman, with lots of tattoos and an improbable thatch of blond hair, talking to two cops. She was making what cops call chicken-head movements with her head, and on her grimy feet, rubber flip-flops danced nervously on the sidewalk. In her thin denim jacket, she was shivering in the cold. Her cheap T-shirt and tight leggings were stretched over her body like sausage casing. When she opened her mouth to draw on her cigarette, I saw the black lipstick and turned away. Snow White had been homecoming queen the year I graduated from Santimoke High School; she had been a terrific singer, and we all thought she was headed for fame and fortune when she'd taken off for Baltimore.

Now she was back, a failed rock star who seemed to eke out a precarious life singing in local bars, although I had heard rumors that she was turning tricks out of her room to supplement that precarious income.

Until now I'd thought they were just ugly rumors. I felt sicker at that moment than I had when I saw the corpse on the bathroom floor, knowing she'd blown whatever dreams she had so she could end up at the Lock and Load.

I walked to the other side of the ambulance so she wouldn't see me. My presence would have been just one more humiliation. For which one of us, I wasn't sure.

"Did you know the deceased?" one cop was asking her.

"Ask Rolley Shallcross," Snow was saying. "He's, like, a manager, you know? He comes around, like, you know, every week to collect the rent, but try to get anything fixed around here, you know, and he's, like, loooong gone. He doesn't, like, live here, you know, and he's never, like, in the office, you know.''

She said a lot more, but none of it made a lot of sense; she was rambling on and on in the way of the stoned.

While I was watching the paramedics fill out forms, I noticed out of the corner of my eye that a door down the court was opening and a familiar head was peering out from right to left and back again.

''Hello, Rig!'' I called loudly, just as my editor thought the coast was clear and he could sneak, undetected, to his car. ''And Jolene! Fancy meeting you all here!'' I sang out loudly.

Jolene's enormous mass of golden hair preceded her out the door. Jolene's hair, you understand, has not just a whole life of its own but a zip code. She was still buttoning her blouse as she appeared, her coat hanging on her shoulders. I would have given anything to have a photograph of their faces as they took in the cops, the ambulances, and me. Their worst nightmare was coming true.

''Whatever brings you two to Room 20 at the Lock and Load?'' I asked sweetly as I walked toward them, tripping over the broken glass and the asphalt chunks. ''I'm out here covering a death in Room 13. You don't know anything about it, do you? Because the police would love it if you did!''

Rig turned the sickly gray color of a Lock and

Load bedsheet, and the mole in the middle of his forehead shone bright red. His hands automatically went to his fly, and the look he gave me should've left the day's second corpse right there on the asphalt.

Jolene's blue eye shadow was smeared across the bridge of her nose, and her mascara was rimming her eyes with raccoon rings.

"Why, H-Hollis," she stammered, teetering uncertainly on her stiletto heels.

"What did you say you were doing here?" Rig demanded.

At that moment the paramedics decided to leave in a wail of sirens, and my reply was lost forever.

". . . and what did you say *you* were doing here?" I asked sweetly.

"We're undercover," Jolene said suddenly. It was probably the one bright idea she'd had in a lifetime. Too bad it didn't fly.

I could have made a thousand nasty puns, but I just grinned evilly. Rig knew and I knew that I finally had him dead to rights, and Rig knew that I knew that Mrs. Riggle would love to know about his "undercover" work at the Lock and Load.

Amateurs, Rig and Jolene. The Lock and Load has seen its share of interesting events. When the cruisers come and the sirens wail, you can bet the regulars stay in their own rooms behind locked doors until the cops go away again. I felt sorry for Snow, who had evidently been in the wrong place at the wrong time yet again.

"Say, Hollis, can you come over here for a minute?" Harve asked me. "Sarge wants to talk to you."

Rig and Jolene saw their moment and took it. They jumped into their cars and sped out of the parking lot, heading back to the *Gazette* to do spin control before I could get there.

They should have relaxed, as far as the newsroom rats were concerned. The more time they spend doing whatever they do (there are some things mankind was not meant to contemplate, and Rig Riggle's sex life is one of them), the less they could screw up the paper.

Still, little-known facts about well-known people have always been a hobby of mine, and I figured this was good for at least six months of Riggle-free writing.

"Hey!" Harve yelled at their departing cars. "We didn't get a chance to question you yet!"

I was happy to give him their tag numbers. Ordinarily, I don't believe in ratting people out, but I thought it would be interesting to hear what Rig came up with when the police came round to question him about leaving the scene of a crime against express orders of law enforcement. And I bet Mrs. Rig would too.

"Say, Harve, who is the stiff? Friendly tossed me before I could find out," I cajoled. "Come on, man, quid pro quo; I just gave you something."

Harve's gold tooth glittered when he smiled one of his rare smiles. The man is painfully earnest. "Sarge told me you'd try that. Come on, Hollis, Orm's my rabbi. I'm not rattin' him out."

I shrugged. "Can't blame a girl for tryin', can ya?" I asked philosophically.

"What's goin' on here? Is she causin' trouble again? I run a clean, respectable place here, and I don't want any trouble!" A shrill voice cut across the cold air.

Harve's attention was claimed by Elvis Man. I noted with interest that Shallcross's elaborate pompadour was sliding to one side of his head.

Harve raised his eyebrows. "Aw, Elvis Man, what's wrong?" he asked.

"I manage this place. What's goin' on here? Who are these people? Is that a reporter? You! With the notebook!" he yelled at me, getting all red in the face. "You're trespassing! No reporters here! I don't need any troublemakers!" As he spoke he rolled up and down on the balls of his tiny feet, giving him the look of a bouncing doll. "Out! Out!" he yelled at me, getting right up in my face so I could see the veins in his nose and smell the tuna on his breath.

But I was so spellbound by him that I barely heard his shrieking voice.

"Arrest her! There's been enough bad press about my motel! This is a clean, respectable place! It's not substandard housing, not a slum like the damned

newspaper said! I want her arrested for criminal trespass!''

I wasn't listening to what Harve said to calm the
little man down, but it must have worked, because
Shallcross turned the color of sour milk and the two
of them wandered back into Room 13.

I soon had other things on my mind.

''Hollis? Hollis Ball?'' Snow White peered at me
through red-rimmed eyes as she huddled inside her
jacket against the wind.

''Snow!'' I exclaimed girlishly, as if we'd just run
into each other at the class reunion. ''I haven't seen
you in years! How are you?''

''How the hell do you think I am?'' she asked. Up
close she smelled sour, like a laundry basket full of
old underwear. I could tell by the flat look she gave
me that she wasn't fooled by me any more than I was
by her. ''Yeah,'' she added matter-of-factly, ''I look
like hell, I know. Late gig last night.'' Before I could
ask her what kind of a gig, she cast an appraising eye
over my ever-so-tasteful business drag—jacket,
sweater, and slacks ensemble—and curled her lip.
''You look so . . . straight!'' she finally concluded.
It wasn't a compliment.

''Just a working girl,'' I replied tightly. Her mock-
ing gaze made me as uncomfortable as her improbable grunge-princess haircut.

She finally laughed. ''Yeah, that's us, just working
girls,'' she cackled. She skunked another cigarette out

of the crumbling pack and fired it up. The smell of tobacco smoke filled the air, and I inhaled longingly.

"You want one?" she asked.

"Let's go around the corner," I said. "If Friendly sees me smoking, he'll kill me. I'm supposed to have stopped. But every once in a while, I smoke an O.P."

"O.P.?"

"Other People's. My favorite brand."

Snow smiled. "Everyone's got a jones for something," she said matter-of-factly. "I'm in 18. Welcome to my world."

Her room was as tattered as 13, but she had added some homey touches to the battered furniture and the grim gray paint. A double wedding-ring quilt was spread across the sagging bed, and she had decorated the walls with posters of Kurt Cobain and Evan Dando and, surprisingly, Phish. Photos of her performing in defunct clubs like the old Marble Bar stood in cheap plastic frames on the nightstand. Her guitar, a battered Epiphone, stood propped up by the wall beside a decrepit Pig Nose amp. A stack of paperbacks covered with voluptuous women in the embrace of well-muscled men lined the little shelf above the Formica table. Instant coffee, powdered milk, sugar, salt, and a handful of spices were placed neatly beside an electric frying pan. The room smelled of peach potpourri and marijuana.

She sat down in one of the plastic chairs, and I sat in the other. *Hapless Hearts,* everyone's favorite soap, was on the flickering TV. I lit a cigarette and inhaled gratefully as Snow studied the screen for a minute. "I read that whole thing in the paper you wrote about Carla Devane on the stories, only her real name is Jennifer Clinton and she used to live around here," Snow offered through a haze of smoke. "I guess you meet a lot of interesting people, huh?"

"Those things will kill you." Sam materialized on the bed. He shook his finger at me angrily. Of course, Snow couldn't see him. "There is," he added smugly, "nothing stupider than a white person with dreads. Tell her the look don't work."

I blew smoke in his direction. It went right through him. He looked around. "What a dump," he said, then laughed. "Damn, I always wanted to say that!" He studied his hostess with interest but said nothing. Somehow, for once in my life, I was glad he was there. Frankly, she scared the hell out of me. I could see her killing me for the price of a pack of Marlboros.

Snow twisted a bit of stringy hair around her finger. Her hands were covered with cheap silver rings; she even had one on her thumb. "I guess you think this place is pretty cheesy, huh?" she asked me sullenly.

The cigarette didn't taste as good as it should have. I felt faintly nauseated. "So, who was the guy in 13?" I asked.

Snow laughed, then turned deadly serious. "Listen, you got any money?'' she asked, scratching a tattoo of a heart and dagger on her forearm.

"Not so you can buy drugs with it."

"Come on, girl. I'm hungry!" she whined. "Give me a break, willya? The welfare cut me off; my last old man, the drummer, beat the crap outta me and took off for Cumberland with a seventeen-year-old. I get a gig where I can, but what'm I supposed to do? I gotta live, so I turn a trick once in a while, okay?"

I opened up my purse and took out some cheese crackers I keep in there for emergencies. She opened the cellophane with her teeth and pushed the orange stuff into her mouth.

"I guess she was hungry," Sam offered. I ignored him. There was nothing a slick ghost could add to this scene.

"Listen," she said, leaning forward. "I've seen and done some really weird shit, right? But this Bang Bang guy was, like, totally weird. I mean, like, beyond weird."

"Kinky?"

Sam sat up, all interest now.

"No, not like you mean." Snow brushed me away with an impatient gesture. "I mean he was dressed up like Elvis, and he wanted me to call him Elvis. I mean, it was like he thought he really was Elvis and not some john from Baltimore. He had the suit and everything! Get this: He wanted me to wear white cotton underpants while I was, you know, doing him.''

"Now, that,'' Sam said, "is really kinky. I've heard of drag queens, but never a drag King.''

"He was dressed up like Elvis?'' I repeated, with a dirty look at Sam, who was rolling on the bed behind Snow, laughing at his own joke. I wondered that she couldn't hear him, but mercifully, she couldn't. Sometimes, pretending you know less than you do is very effective.

Snow nodded. She sucked at her cigarette and, with her little finger, dabbed at the cracker crumbs around her mouth. "Innit that the weirdest thing you ever heard?'' she demanded flatly. "I've had some damned strange requests, but that one sure kicked the shit out of me.''

"So, did you?''

She shrugged. "Sure. Why not? But you know, he, like, passed out before he paid me, so this morning I went back to collect what he owed me and I seen him dead on the floor. So I took my fifty dollars outta his wallet.''

"And you hooked his wallet too.''

Snow shrugged. "I gave it back, didn't I?'' she asked, scratching her arms.

"Were you taking those pills with him?''

"What pills?'' Snow asked blankly. "He didn't have any pills.''

Whether she was lying or not wasn't my problem.
"So, did you see his name in his wallet?"

"Yeah. It was, like, really weird. Look, here, I got
his MasterCard. Take a look for yourself."

She pulled it out of her pocket.

I read the name embossed on the plastic.

ALBANUS L. LYDEKKER
B and B Enterprises

"Albie!" I yelped.

Snow brightened. "Oh, do you know Albie too?"
she asked.

Sam collapsed on the bed with nary a wrinkle to
the quilt. "You shoulda known, Holl!" He sighed,
then disappeared in a puff of smoke.

5

ALL SHOOK UP

"ALBIE LYDEKKER? THE SAME ALBIE Lydekker who played for the Birds back in the sixties? He's your godfather?" Friendly asked, either impressed or incredulous, I couldn't tell which. Albie was the only one in chambers; Frank had ducked out for a conference with his law clerk, Albie'd told us. My godfather's solitaire game was laid out on the table. Doubtless, he was cheating on himself.

"Guilty as charged," Albie said agreeably. He gave Friendly a hearty handshake that made the big cop wince. "And you're Hollis's boyfriend?" he demanded.

Friendly smiled. "You could say we're dating," he agreed cautiously, with a sideways look at me. Our path to romance is a bumpy one, often complicated, so who knows what we are today?

Albie eyed him narrowly. "So, you're divorced, right?" he queried. "How many times?"

"Albie!" I protested, embarrassed.

"Twice," Friendly said, not visibly discomfited. "You?"

"Depends on if the last one was legal or not, since I wasn't quite divorced from the one before that." Albie grinned. "I guess three, four times."

"Five, Albie," I reminded him. "Anyway, this isn't about Friendly. This is about you."

"Moi?" Albie blinked innocently. He laid a card down on the table.

"Yeah. Seems like your wallet and ID turned up on a dead man at the Lock and Load Motor Inn this morning." Friendly looked at him quizzically.

Albie didn't even blink. He patted his rear pocket and withdrew a battered leather billfold. "Say," he said in tones of elaborate surprise. "This ain't my wallet!"

"Would you open it, please, and withdraw any identification you might find in there?" Friendly asked, all businesslike.

Albie did as he was commanded. When he looked at the driver's license he found there, he made a moue of astonishment, his mouth as round as a doughnut. "Say! This is Bang Bang's wallet!" he exclaimed handing it to Friendly.

That was the moment I had been dreading. "Albie, what *are* you doing with Bang Bang Devine's wallet?" I demanded. "What are you up to now?"

My godfather shrugged. "They musta gotten mixed up yesterday morning when I met him out to the Lock and Load."

"Are you staying at the Lock and Load, Mr. Lydekker?" Friendly asked.

Albie nodded. "I was. But I slept in the county jail last night." He grinned unrepentantly at Friendly, who grinned right back.

Not a good sign. Oh, Albie, I thought, please don't screw with Friendly; he'll eat you alive. I had to remind myself that this was a potential homicide investigation. Potential, until the M.E.'s office made an official ruling, though that didn't make it any less scary. Of course, I couldn't have been there if it was official. But Friendly needed me just to find Albie, so I was in.

"You know Bang Bang Devine, huh?" He grinned at Albie.

"He and I are bidness partners," Albie replied.

If he wasn't going to give up the thing about the gambling debt, neither was I. Albie had no idea how bad this was starting to look.

Friendly produced a Polaroid snapshot of the late great Bang Bang as the man had looked this morning. "This him?" he asked casually.

Albie squinted at it, then nodded. "Yeah," he

agreed. "Say, he don't look too good, does he? He's not sick, is he? Where's this going? I thought you came over here so I could meet your boyfriend, Hollis."

"Calm down, Albie. You're not in any trouble."

Yet. Come to think of it, I couldn't think of a time when Albie wasn't in trouble.

Friendly leaned in toward Albie. "Bang Bang was found dead in his room at the motel this morning."

Albie blanched beneath his freckles, then flushed up to the roots of his hair. He made a whistling sound between his front teeth. "Damn," he said. "You sure?"

"Well, we'll need the next of kin to make a positive ID at the M.E.'s office, but it looks like his photo ID and the deceased match up. What was the notorious Bang Bang Devine doing on the Eastern Shore, Albie?"

Since Friendly had been exiled from Baltimore to the Shore by the Big Giant Head at M.S.P., he knew all about Bang Bang Devine.

"He's legit, Sergeant." Albie spread out his fingers on the top of the table. "He's strictly legit these days. He *was,* anyway. Damn! I can't believe he's dead! Room 13 at the Cocky Locky?"

"Dead as a doornail," I said. "And dressed in an—"

Friendly's big old foot came down gently on top of my own under the table. I shut up, but I didn't want to. I knew, even if Friendly didn't, that Albie had gotten himself into a whole world of shit, but he had nothing to do with drugs or pills or murder. Gambling, not homicide, was Albie's addiction of preference. "What brought him to the Eastern Shore?"

"Well," Albie drawled, not looking at me. "He was here to see about setting up a gambling casino where the old canneries are, down by the water."

"B and B Enterprises!" I exclaimed. "Bang and Bang! But Albie, you told me it was just an Elvis contest."

Albie didn't look at me. "Well, we thought the tribute artists' contest would be good public relations for the casino," he muttered, looking at his size-13 shoes.

"And you were going to sucker me and Frank into being judges for *that*? Albie, that would make it appear that we endorsed gambling in Santimoke County! You know we can't do that! Neither a judge nor a journalist can make a public political statement! Jesus, Albie, what were you thinking?"

"I was thinkin' that I didn't want to get my legs broken, that's what." Albie slumped in his chair.

"Why would Bang Bang want to break your legs?" Friendly asked gently.

"Tell him the truth, Albie," I warned.

Albie's big old freckled hands twisted on the table in front of him. "Well, I was into him for a lot of money," he finally admitted.

"Gambling debts?"

"He doesn't have to answer that," I said.

Friendly gave me his crooked grin. "Don't lawyer me, Hollis," he advised genially.

"Look, I let you talk to Albie because you needed to ID the body," I complained. "He's my godfather! I know he wouldn't hurt a fly!" It sounded trite even as I heard it coming out of my mouth.

"Nobody said anything about hurtin' anyone," Friendly countered flatly. The look he shot me could have peeled my paint, if I peeled easily, which I don't. "Now, Mr. Lydekker, in your experience did Bang Bang take a lot of pills? Uppers? Downers? Painkillers? Stuff like that?"

Albie shrugged. "Not so much as you'd notice, I guess," he offered. "I mean, I never seen 'im pop nothing too much." He brightened a little. "But I mind my own bidness—you know?"

Friendly nodded. "No Percodan, Darvon, stuff like that?"

Albie turned up the palms of his hands. "Hey, I don't party with the dude, you know? It was strictly business with us."

"How could you use Frank and me?" I demanded. "Damn, Albie, that is so cold!"

Friendly's green eyes flickered at me, but he said nothing, merely scribbled down some notes.

"Aw, Holly, honey, I woulda figgered something out!" he assured me. "I didn't know you all couldn't do it. Anyway, I guess it was a moot point all the way. The county council turned down Bang Bang's ideas. They can't see a big ole redbrick colonial casino down at the waterfront, and of course I told Bang they wouldn't, but he don't unnerstan' Eastern Shore folk.'' Albie cast a significant look at Friendly. ''He's from Bawlmore.''

''It's not a region, it's a cult,'' Friendly agreed. ''I could see how Bang Bang wouldn't get it. He was a city boy through and through.'' He gave Albie one of his disarming grins.

Boy, I thought, this is a battle of the testosterone bands.

''Did Bang Bang have any enemies?'' Friendly asked.

Both of them laughed at that question. But friendly wiped the grin off his face swiftly. ''Becuase it looks,'' he continued, eyeing Albie, ''as if somebody strangled Bang Bang last night.''

Albie blinked. His hands clutched at the cards on the table. ''You sayin' Bang Bang didn't OD?'' he asked. ''Somebody killed him?''

Friendly nodded.

Albie licked his lips. ''Oh, man.'' He sighed.

''Do you know anything about why Bang Bang Devine was found dead on the bathroom floor at the Lock and Load, wearing an Elvis suit and a thin red scarf wrapped tightly around his neck? So tightly it strangled him?'' Friendly leaned forward, showing him a second photo of the late Bang Bang, this time on his back.

Albie looked, winced, shook his head. "I don't know anything about it."

I believed him.

But Friendly pressed on with a couple more questions about Albie's whereabouts. When Albie told him the same thing three times, Cop Boy gave up.

"An airtight alibi and a foolproof plan," Friendly growled. "It's everyone's wet dream."

"Is that all you want from me, Sergeant?" Albie asked with an elaborate glance at his watch.

"For now, yeah. Someone in Baltimore will call Mrs. Devine and have her come down to Penn Street and ID Bang Bang. But thanks for your time. It's a real pleasure to meet a guy who played with the O's." Friendly thrust out his hand again and Albie gripped it. Hard.

"I think you'd better stick around for a while," Friendly added through clenched teeth. "In case we need to get a hold of you."

"Oh, I ain't goin' nowhere," Albie promised. "I've got to get the cocktail lounge at the Lock and Load set up for the contest. What Albie Lydekker starts, Albie Lydekker finishes."

"You wouldn't mind comin' out to the barracks to make a statement, would you?" Friendly asked.

Albie touched the side of his nose. "I am always

ready to assist the police in any way possible," he said grandly, rising from his chair.

"Shovel, please," I muttered, burying my head in my hands.

AFTER THEY LEFT FOR THE BARRACKS, I GOT UP AND made my rounds through the courthouse. I checked the charging documents, and sure enough, Albie was there, along with a couple of DWI's and a drug bust on Back Street. I went past the county sheriff's office, then, as I was headed toward district court, I saw Judge Helen Quick and State's Attorney Athena "Hardass" Hardcastle, who watched me loping down the hall and started to laugh.

"Elvis!" they both exclaimed.

"How did you get roped into that?" Helen gasped between chuckles, waving her glasses at me.

"Elvis? Elvis? *Elvis!*" Athena hooted at me. "Girlfriend, what have you done now?"

"Well," I said uncertainly. "See, Albie Lydekker is my godfather—"

"Albie Lydekker?" Helen exclaimed. "Oh, Hollis, I am so sorry, dear."

"Albie Lydekker who pitched for the '66 Orioles?" Athena asked. She loves those Birds as a good Baltimoron should.

"That Albie Lydekker," I reassured them gloomily. I was getting a little tired of having to defend him by that point. But of course I had to tell them all about the events of the day, which was fine until I mentioned that the corpse was Bang Bang Devine.

"Bang Bang?" Athena frowned, suddenly grave. "The Devines are old-time players, Hollis, and Bang Bang was the worst of the lot, a real thug." She squeezed my shoulder. "Look, white girl, I'm telling you as your friend, those Devines are bad news. You stay out of that mess, you hear me, girl? I don't want to see you end up at the bottom of the Bay attached to a transmission like Crabby Devine."

I think she was serious. Athena doesn't joke about criminal behavior.

So I WENT BACK UPSTAIRS AND PUT MY HEAD BACK IN my hands again, which was how Frank found me when he returned from his afternoon court session. I had to relate the whole sorry story all over again.

"Ugh," Frank said. As he listened to me pour out my latest tale of woe, he filled the bird feeder on his window with scraps of sandwich left from his lunch. Very soon Edgar Allan Crow, who lives in the vine trellis on the courthouse wall, perched on the sill to feed. Edgar kicked aside a pickle with a look of contempt and went to work on some chicken salad with his black beak. "Naw. Maw," he announced, taking a break before eyeing a tomato suspiciously. Edgar is a fish crow, by the way, and smarter than many humans I know.

Frank leaned against the window frame and looked out across the street, his bushy eyebrows pulled together. "Bang Bang Devine," he mused. "Now, there's a name I haven't heard for a while. Nasty piece of work, just like his old man, Crabby Devine."

"Albie's into Bang Bang for ten thousand dollars. And now Bang Bang is dead. This doesn't look good, does it?"

"Where Albie Lydekker is concerned, nothing ever looks good, except to Albie," Frank observed mildly. He was a lot less upset than I thought he would be. "Personally, I don't much care for legalized gambling; I think it's easy to view it as a quick fix for local economic problems, when in reality it creates a whole new set of issues—and crimes." He used his thumb and forefinger to rub the bridge of his nose. "My docket's already clogged up with drug cases. I don't need to add prostitution, more drugs, and more crime to the mix."

"I saw Snow White today," I said dreamily.

"I don't want to know, do I?" Frank thought for a moment. You could almost see him mentally flipping through his dockets. "She got popped for soliciting, didn't make her court date, so she's in contempt of court. She's got an F.T.A. on her, I think. You could check and see if Bry's served a warrant on her for failure to appear. That's a sad case. Kid had talent. What ruined her? Drugs?''

"I guess, if you say so." Keeping up with Snow's rap sheet wasn't at the top of my list of priorities. Right now being involved, however indirectly, with what could become a political mess was. If she was in trouble with her parole officer or had outstandings or a contempt citation, it was none of my business. I couldn't fix the world, and I'd long ago given up trying.

"Well, maybe the whole thing will blow over. If Albie's off the hook, then so are we," Frank observed. "Legally, we're under no obligation to judge anything, since he used our names without our consent. A retraction in the paper will do.''

"Which Rig will bury in the want ads," I offered unhappily.

"Let him try," Frank replied, taking off his glasses and cleaning them with a handkerchief. "I'll call him into chambers and tear him a new body orifice.''

Since Rig has a spine of Jell-O, especially when confronted by anyone who holds power, I could see where this would work. I was just about to allow myself to feel more comfortable when I heard Friendly's voice talking to Jill, Frank's clerk.

I should have known what was up when he and Albie walked into the office, the pair of them grinning like fools.

"Well," Friendly said, "it's a done deal. I'm gonna be the third judge in the Elvis contest. I just love me some Elvis!"

Albie's charm had struck down another victim.

6

HUNK-A HUNK-A BURNIN' LOVE

"I KNOW IT'S IN HERE SOMEWHERE," Friendly muttered, digging in the back of his closet. "I know Marisa didn't want it in the divorce settlement."

"Having an Elvis suit in your possession is probably why she divorced you in the first place," I observed. I'd heard just enough about Marisa to be really curious. But with a ghostly ex-husband as my deepest darkest secret, I wasn't anxious to swap ex-spouse stories, at least not yet.

"I know it's around somewhere," he said, his voice muffled in the clutter.

Friendly lives in one of those prechewed condo complexes that have sprung up around the edges of Watertown. You know the type—that hideous combination of Victorian and colonial that seems to define architectural taste at the *fin* of this god-awful *siècle*. Pastel aluminum siding and paper-thin walls, sad little shrubberies that never survive, and a condo board that fights over parking and the color of your curtains. I have a vast sense that this is the slum property of tomorrow. I hated it, but Friendly couldn't care less where he lived in casual bachelor squalor. The two items of decor he prized the most were his big-screen TV and his recliner, and the first lesson I learned was not to get between Cop Boy and his remote. To say that Friendly was indifferent to his surroundings was the same as saying that Attila the Hun was mildly annoying.

Most of his decorating ideas seemed to involve fishing tackle, hunting gear, and that recliner, all of them in some stage of being cleaned or refurbished or played with. Although I did notice that the cinderblock and plank bookshelves were beginning to fill up with waterfowl decoys, his new collecting passion.

"I never knew you were an Elvis fan," I said. "But then again there's a lot of stuff I don't know about you."

"And there is a lot of stuff I don't know about you," he replied, his voice muffled as a box of back issues of *Maryland Trooper* magazine poured out of the closet and over his head, followed by outboard-motor parts and assorted pieces of athletic equipment.

"But it's fun learning it," he added without missing a beat.

I picked up a jock strap and swung it over my head in a circle, doing a little two-step shuffle. "Miss Santimoke County, Amber Rottweiler, will now demonstrate her talent in her self-choreographed *danse de support d'athlétique*. Miss Rottweiler, a junior at Miss Patti's Christian School of Tap and Ballet, aspires to a career in dog grooming." The elastic belt snapped out of my hand during a *pas de cup* and hit the cedarwood-burl deer-antler clock on the wall, where it stayed. I sat down demurely on the plaid couch. "Well, I hope you noticed that I never pry into the details of your marriage, although I do know that Marisa got the house in Federal Hill and all the furniture—"

"Well, she has kids from her first marriage; she deserved to keep it," Friendly said, ignoring me as he dove deeper into the closet. "And then there's this ex-husband of yours you don't like talking about—"

"Sam is a dead issue," I said quickly. "I wish he were, but no such luck," I muttered under my breath. "Anyway, I'm glad you like Albie."

"Well, he was with the O's; ya gotta like that," Friendly observed as I observed his fine, fine behind bent over a pile of something in the closet.

"Everyone else is furious with him. Mother and Dad won't even speak to him, and Toby banned him forever this morning. They just don't understand—"

"Hunk-a hunk-a burnin' love, baby!"

I watched, open-mouthed, as Elvis emerged from the closet.

Friendly had it down, all right; his white satin jumpsuit had a flange collar embroidered with gold braid and sequins, and foot-long satin fringes dangled from his sleeves and flaring legs. The suit was open to midsternum, revealing his hairy chest and an enormous golden medallion. When he gave me a turn, the back of his suit dazzled with the reflected glory of a gold and silver sunburst. He made a few karate moves and spun so that I could get the full effect of the blue-black, hot buttered yak-wool wig and the silver aviator shades. "I'm-a you' hunk-a hunk-a burnin' love, baby," he growled. "It's left over from the Elvis bust of '86."

"You look like the Spirit of '76!" I howled, collapsing on the couch. "1976!"

Elvis vaulted the back of the settee and collapsed in a heap of glitz on top of me. "Let Elvis into the buildin', darlin'," he rumbled, giving me a big old wet smackeroo.

"You smell like mothballs and stale cologne!" I laughed, but I kissed him back, allowing him to gather me up in his arms like the cover of a paperback romance and sweep me off to the bedroom without stopping to think about the consequences to his back.

"Hunk-a hunk-a burnin' loooooove," he wheezed. "That's not mothballs, that's Brut, ma favorite cologne, darlin' . . . whooo! The King ain't used to liftin' his teddy bear—''

"The King is gonna have a king-size hernia—" I started to say, and then things got more interesting and I didn't have anything to say that I am going repeat here, except to say that whatever else Ormand Friendly is, he is *never* boring.

"Ladies and gentlemen," my beau crowed, "Elvis has entered the building!"

"WELL! WHERE HAVE YOU BEEN?" SAM ASKED IRRITA - bly.

My key was still in the door, but I didn't have to flip on the light switch to see the form of my ex sitting at my kitchen table. He glowed in the dark, his arms crossed, a sullen frown on his handsome face.

"Since you spend all your time in my business," I said, flipping on the kitchen light, "you know that I was at Friendly's place."

Under the hard illumination Sam became more solid, but he was still an interesting shade of red. Venus, the Cat with an Attitude, jumped up on the kitchen table, rubbing herself affectionately through his shoulder and meowing loudly at me for food, which will tell you something about my cat's taste in people.

I opened a can of Super Supper and ladled it into Venus's dish. She jumped off the table and chowed down. I turned the light off again and watched as Sam began to glow like deep-sea shrimp.

"You know," I said, "when you do that you look like a nuclear reactor. Or a Lava lamp. Or one of those glow-in-the-dark Virgin Mary plates you can order from *TV Guide.*"

Sam turned up his wattage; his glow began to illuminate the whole kitchen. It was sort of weird, but, then, what's *not* weird about having a ghost around?

I dug a diet Pepsi out of the refrigerator and popped the top, watching as he passed from an angry red into a hot pink, then to a sort of lavender, finally ending up blue. "Nice trick," I offered. "You look like a Jimi Hendrix poster."

Sam is nothing if not easily distracted, which is how he got himself dead in the first place. "Cool, huh?" he asked complacently, watching his own hand go from blue to green to a sunny yellow. "The longer I'm dead, the better I like this ghost stuff."

"Personally, I'd like to be haunted by the Gray Lady of Stately Hollis Manor, but you can't have everything." I took off my coat and threw it across the back of a chair. "Or better yet, the Gray Butler of Stately Hollis Manor. He'd have brought in the wood and started a fire in the stove, at least. And have my Pepsi and slippers waiting by the fire with a single Reese's Cup on a silver platter."

"I live to serve." Sam sighed as he picked up my coat and hung it in the closet, acting as if this were a big favor, which it may be for an ectoplasmic being. Unfortunately my coat kept slipping *through* his hands. Finally, he materialized a bit and got a hold on it. Then he sniffed at it, wrinkling his nose. "Is that Brut I smell?" he demanded in suspicious tones.

I made a great production out of feeding the wood-stove. While I was moving logs from the basket into the Nordic King, Sam floated along beside me, sniffing at my hair and my clothes. "It is Brut!" he exclaimed. "My God, Hollis, have you been seeing another ghost?"

I crumbled up old newspaper around the logs, and Sam zapped it with a snap of his fingers, which is one of his few stupid ghost tricks that is really useful. A cheerful fire began to flare up.

"No, of course not," I replied, carefully avoiding his gaze. "Friendly's got an Elvis outfit, and it smells like Brut," I admitted. "Real stale Brut." I drew circles on the side of my Pepsi can.

Sam glowed pinkly, like a sunset. "So, that's where you've been," he said sullenly.

"Well, he doesn't like to come here because he thinks my house is haunted. Not that he believes in ghosts, of course, but I think he's afraid of them anyway." I drew more circles.

"You're sleeping with a man who owns an Elvis suit? And he wears Brut? Holl, how could you?"

"Well, I didn't know he had an Elvis suit until tonight. And he doesn't wear Brut. Elvis does. Did.

The suit—and the Brut—were left over from a drug bust. Don't ask—I didn't.''

"Believe me, I don't want to know," Sam said. He was turning an interesting shade of green.

"You're jealous!" I exclaimed. "Why, Sam! You're pea green with envy!''

"No, I'm not!" Sam exclaimed, floating gently off the floor and rising toward the ceiling like an angry balloon.

"Denial ain't a river in Egypt!" I crowed unkindly. Actually, it was rather nice to get my own back on Sam, since he's gotten over so many times on me since his untimely demise. I drew more circles to fill the ensuing silence. "Why do you dislike Friendly so much, then? He's a perfectly decent human being. It's not like we have a major commitment or anything; we've taken this whole thing at a crawl because we've both been hurt pretty bad by previous people, which in my case would include your lovely self.''

"Touché," Sam said huffily. He gave me his profile, and while it is a handsome profile indeed, it left me unmoved. He cast me a look out of the side of his eye. "Still and all, while I haunt around this cold house, with only the cat for company, you're out having fun.''

"Fun into which you pop at every inopportune moment," I reminded him. "And then things aren't so much fun anymore. You're the life and death of every party, Sambo.''

"Not *every* inopportune moment," Sam retorted with a sneer.

"You wouldn't! You didn't!" I exclaimed, horrified. "You couldn't!"

Sam grinned. "I could, if I wanted to," he chuckled.

"You are *so* immature!" I was yelling, but I didn't care. "It's a good thing you're dead, because if you weren't I'd have to kill you right now! Why don't you get a life?"

"I had one, if you recall," Sam said with a wounded dignity that didn't fool me for one minute.

" 'But you are in a wheelchair, Blanche,' " I snarled. When I start quoting old movies, I know I'm approaching the end of my sad, frayed rope. "When we were married you made it damned and all clear that commitment wasn't your thing. Now that you're dead you suddenly want to poke and pry and critique my life?"

Sam slowly floated down from the ceiling until he was at my eye level. He was turning purple, then blue. "Look, Holl," he said in a maddeningly reasonable tone of voice, "it's all about this mess with Albie. You know what Albie's like, and you know in your heart that this is going to be another fiasco. And this time I might not be able to get you out of it."

"So now you're going to act like Mother and Dad and Toby and start up on Albie. Jeez, Sam, not you too. None of you understands him, that's all." I rolled my eyes. "I always thought you of all people would understand how I feel about Albie."

"I do, all too well," Sam replied evenly. He stretched out in midair and took a deep breath. He slowly returned to normal colors. "Look, Holl, it's my ghostly job to protect you from getting into trouble. And Albie is trouble with a capital *T*."

"But every time I get into a mess, you've dragged me into it!" I pointed out defensively. "I'm just rolling along, minding my own business, and then you pop up and the next thing I know, I'm in a whole world of trouble!"

"Be that as it may," Sam said dismissively. "But this time I'm warning you that you should stay away from Albie and this Elvis contest thing. You're dealing with forces that you don't understand, Hollis."

"What? Aliens from Uranus? Werewolves? Vampires? Satan?"

"No, the Devine family," he replied in utter seriousness.

"Oh, what the pluperfect hell! Bang Bang's dead! He can't hurt Albie now. Sam, you are so manipulative! I thought you'd understand—you and Albie are just alike!"

"Holl, listen to me. I'm as serious as a heart attack! You're playing with some bad company. You don't know the half of it!"

I was tired, I was disgusted. Alive or dead, Sam's skill at pushing my buttons was making me angry.

And I was sick of everyone dissing Albie. Sam, of all folk living or dead, should have understood.

I blew up.

"I've had just about enough of you, Sam! Why don't you go rattle some chains or find someone who cares? Just get out of here! Go away! I don't want to see you anymore!"

Sam righted himself. He turned a dark blue and gave me a long, hard look. But I didn't back down. "Just go away!" I yelled.

"Okay. Okay," Sam said softly. "I'll do that. Good-bye, Hollis."

And with that, he disappeared.

"And don't come back!" I yelled into thin air. For comfort I reached out to pet Venus, but she raised her tail and, head high, marched out of the room.

The house suddenly seemed very empty and alone.

And that suited me just fine, thank you.

7

GOT MY MOJO WORKING

♪ ♪ LIKE A CREEPING VIRUS, ALBIE'S POSTERS began to appear all over town. Every store window, every bulletin board, every phone pole seemed to have sprouted a silver and blue Elvis poster, beckoning the public to come to a night of magic, or at least of mild interest.

And from the way the public reacted, you'd think that it mattered desperately. Albie must have been thrilled. I knew he was out there, for like the Lone Ranger, he left his mark everywhere he went.

"Who was that masked man, Lucinda?"

"I don't know, Ray Bob, but he left this silver poster."

And believe it or not, the great unwashed public responded. People who used to stop me in the Buy

'N' Bag to harangue me about the way the paper covered the news (hey, lady, sorry about your junkie son holding up a gas station with a hand grenade, but I just report it) now started to waylay me by the Poultry Packers to discuss their personal feelings about Elvis and his tribute artists. After a while I began to wish they'd go back to yelling at me about the news.

"I think it's just awful! I mean, let the man rest in peace," one well-dressed man huffed.

"You know, Elvis isn't really dead," a kindly blue-haired lady confided in me. "He just couldn't handle the pressure of all that fame, and he faked his own death so he could lead a normal life. I know, because I saw him at a Burger King in Elmwood, Ontario."

"I don't understand why you people don't do something about Jesus!" The woman's curlers bobbed on her scalp as she shook her finger at me. "Jesus is who you need to do something about! We need a whole lot more of Jesus and a lot less rock and roll! We'd beat Satan's nonsense out of you with a Bible at my church!" she hissed, getting right up in my face.

"You're absolutely right! Let's put the fun back into fundamentalism," I replied sweetly.

But a lot of people just wanted to know where they could sign up. I had no idea there were so many wannabe Elvii on the Eastern Shore; they were coming out of the closet and the woodwork.

"Hey, Hollis!" Big Tuna Scroggins called as he

came loping up to me in the Horny Mallard at lunch-time. "Check it out!" He produced a pair of aviator shades and gave me a couple of Elvis's patented ka-rate moves. They don't call the man Big Tuna for nothing; he's got a thyroid condition that makes him look like a fish. A big fish. Tuna and Toby used to be quarterbacks together at Santimoke High. Don't ask.

"Lemme guess," I said to the big guy. "Bail Bond Elvis?"

"You got it," he beamed. "Elvis puts your feet back on the street. Only I've got my own special take on the thing." He turned around, then with a hideous leer leaned closer to me so I could see the plastic fangs he'd added to his bridgework. "Drac-Elvis. Elvis as a vampire, get it? It'll kill the Anne Rice fans!"

"Vampire Elvis?" I repeated weakly.

"Drac-Elvis. The King of Rock and Roll Dark-ness!" Big Tuna lisped around his new incisors. "I vant to suck your rock and roll blood!"

"It's a plan," I managed to say.

Pleased by my reaction, Big Tuna spit out his fangs. "Speaking of back on the street, and we were, drop by the office and get your bond back." He twitched out a wink. "Seems like Mrs. Vera Devine blew into town last night and took over Albie's case."

"Vera Devine?" I gulped, almost choking on my Mallardburger.

Big Tuna nodded cheerfully. "Yeah, Vera Deevine. And she is, and she is.'' He grinned. ''A real baby doll, that one.'' Having used the Eastern Shore man's highest accolade for feminine beauty, he jammed his fangs back into his mouth and winked at me. He looked like a catfish.

''Mrs. Bang Bang.'' Not only was my reporter sense tingling, but icy fingers were doing the tango up and down my spine. And since Sam was on the outs with me, it wasn't that old black magic. Or so I thought.

Suddenly, it explained why Albie hadn't been returning my calls. Vera, no doubt a hardened, big-haired, married-to-the-mob girl, was holding him directly responsible for the unfortunate demise of her late great hubby, Bang Bang. Perhaps even at that moment she was encasing Albie's size-13 feet in a tub of concrete and gunning up the boat to drop him off in the Baltimore Shipping Channel.

My duty was clear. ''Put that on my tab, Donna!'' I yelled as I ran for my car. I came back and grabbed my cheeseburger, however. No sense battling gangsters on an empty stomach.

THE LOCK AND LOAD MOTOR INN LOOKED LIKE IT ALways does. Really, really depressing. Trash blew across the asphalt, and the sad, broken-down cars seemed to sag in their spaces. I had the feeling that a lot of people were watching me behind drawn curtains, and some of them were probably armed and dangerous.

Tattered yellow tape still crisscrossed the doorway of Room 13. I was willing to bet that the minute the cops had left, Lock and Load residents had scavenged the room like rats on a new load at the landfill, liberating anything that wasn't nailed down.

I pulled up beside a brand-new Volvo with a bumper sticker that advised random acts of kindness can lead to senseless beauty. Probably a yuppie type looking to score. It looked as out of place here as Queen Elizabeth in a drunk tank.

I carefully locked all my doors before I went to pound on the door of Room 12. I fully expected to find Albie tied to a chair, being beaten black and blue by thugs wearing gold chains and lots of polyester.

Happily, my .38 was jammed into the bottom of my pocketbook along with my cell phone and two pounds of loose Altoids. I was prepared for anything from murder to bad breath.

I closed my fingers around the grip and pushed on the door.

"Albie!" I called and barged on in, ready to rescue my hapless godfather once again.

For a moment I couldn't see anything for the thick cloud of incense that permeated the tiny room.

But it didn't look like Albie needed any rescuing at all. He was stretched out nude beneath a sheet on a long table, while a fortyish woman with a long, untamed mass of curly hair and a whole gift shop full of bead necklaces and bracelets was working him over with some heavy-smelling oil. Little bits of clear stone were balanced all over his skinny white body: on his forehead, in the palms of his hands, on his feet, his chest, his knees, his—well, you get the idea.

"Hey, Hollis!" Albie said in a faintly annoyed tone. "You're upsetting my aromatherapy session!"

"Deep breaths, deep breaths, Albie," cautioned the woman, shaking her—I swear—deep-purple hair out of her eyes. "Don't loosen the karmic balance! Let your inner child breathe!"

"I'm losin' the moment," Albie grumbled. "My inner child is purely pissed off, Vera. Dammit, Hollis, whyn't you knock when a man's in the middle of his spiritual-balance cleansing?"

"Vera?" I stammered. "*You're* Vera Devine?"

Layers of purple and lavender rayon robes, scarves, and shawls floated out from her thin figure as the Widow Devine turned to respond to her name. In her thick Birkenstock sandals and crunchy rag socks, she had a little trouble being graceful, but she thrust out one be-ringed, henna-painted hand in greeting while she clutched at her massive collection of amber and crystal necklaces with the other, perhaps to retain her balance. She was a little top-heavy with crystals and other sacred stones. By their crystals you shall know them; I was in the presence of a genuine New Age human.

"Peace and love be with you," she said in a reedy voice, assessing me from kohl-rimmed eyes full of New Age bliss. Her limp handshake was greasy with massage oil. Hands that have massaged Albie are not hands I want to touch.

"I'm, uh, so sorry about your husband," I managed to stammer. Once again my preconceptions had led me astray. But who would imagine the Widow Bang Bang as New Age starlet?

Vera Devine gave me a sad, small smile. "Bang Bang has passed into the Great Eternal, where all things must go. My spirit guide tells me he has already been reincarnated."

"As a turnip in Saddlebrook, New Jersey," Albie muttered.

"On the sacred wheel," Vera Devine continued, oblivious, "all things become what they once were and will be again, and this is as it is." She closed her eyes, took a couple of deep breaths, placed the palms of her hands together, and bowed. "All grief is selfishness. Bang Bang chose his own destiny. I have drummed for him, to guide him on his astral path toward a fuller fulfillment of his karma, and my spirit guide has informed me that all is in harmonic balance."

"Your spirit guide?" I repeated stupidly. I'd lost the trail beyond that.

"Hey, I'm getting cold over here!" Albie yelped

from the massage table. "What about my inner child? These crystals are getting awful heavy!"

"Relax, Albie. Let the spirits channel through you. Your *chai* is sadly out of balance. It's probably the poor *fêng shui* of this room." She drew her scarves and shawls about her and shuddered.

"Huh?" Albie grunted.

"The decor does leave something to be desired," I agreed, looking around at the room's faded fifties' ambience.

Vera Devine cocked her head. I didn't like the way she was studying me. It reminded me too much of my mother. "We must dialogue," she said. "Commune in our womanness. Do you journal?"

"No, I'm a journal-ist," I admitted. "Hollis Ball. I'm his goddaughter." I jerked a thumb toward Albie, who was still whining about the rigors of balancing crystals on various parts of his body.

"Oh, you poor dear." Vera Devine sighed.

I thought she meant because of my Albie connection, but she was taking it to a different level entirely. "You know, a ritual fasting and some black-cohosh drops would clear up those dark circles under your eyes."

"So would a good night's sleep," I replied, backing away before she could roll some quartzes over me or make me drink some herb tea or something. Crystal crunchers scare the hell out of me.

"There's really something missing in your life,"

she persisted. "My spirit guide is telling me that your astral-plane companion is out of sync with you."

My reporter sense tingled again. "My what?" I asked, just to be sure.

"Your astral-plane companion. Your spirit guide," Vera explained carefully. She didn't laugh either.

Uh-oh. Maybe Vera Devine, apostle of New Age Fuzzy Bunny Feel Good, was on to something after all?

"Of course, all of us have spirit guides," she continued. "Many prefer to call them angels." She rattled her strands of crystal and amber beads, blowing the moment. "Angels are all around us, you know." She pursed her lips. "My spirit guide is an Old One who has been through a recent earthly life."

"Vera! My massage?" Albie howled. "I'm cold!"

"Patience, my dear. All things come to those who journey the sacred wheel. Cleansing your *chai* of the trauma of Bang Bang's unhappy transition takes time," Vera counseled wisely. "Not everyone is advanced spiritually." She beamed at me. "Bang Bang has transitioned to a better place. But Albie has not transitioned to a higher level of understanding. He needs to cleanse."

"That's not all he needs," I said and got a dirty look from Albie for my pains.

Vera passed her hands over her head and, holding them out to her sides, began to shake them violently. "I'm cleansing myself of negativity," she explained.

"Negative elements are everywhere, especially where untimely death is concerned. This motel is a negative place, sadly. It's full of demons."

"O-kay," I agreed, backing toward the door.

"Wait!" Vera Devine held up a be-ringed hand. "My spirit guide is telling me something." She pursed her lips and frowned, ignoring Albie's whimpering and my obvious desire to get out of the House of the Spirits. "My spirit guide tells me that you would be willing to continue the work that Bang Bang started."

"Lady, I'm not into loan-sharking and gambling—"

"Hist!" she said. She really did. "My spirit guide tells me that you will continue the vision of Elvis tribute that Bang Bang loved so much."

"Does your spirit guide tell you that I don't subscribe to his religion?"

Vera smiled serenely. "He says you'll do it because Albie owes Bang Bang's estate ten thousand of your material world dollars. And if Albie doesn't pay up, he'll incur some really bad karma." She nodded, taking some shallow panting breaths like an overheated retriever, and cleansed herself again.

"Since you put it that way." I sighed.

"Do it, Holly! I'm freezing here!" Albie begged.

So I was back in before I even had a chance to get out.

Vera made short work of finishing up Albie's massage, then instructed him to go take a shower.

"You know," she informed me cheerfully as she wiped her hands with a thin Lock and Load towel, "*you* could really use a balancing treatment." As the Estée Lauder of the Aquarian Age flexed her fingers, I noticed how large her hands were, well-muscled and strong, oddly masculine for such a dainty, drifty woman. "Therapeutic massage and perhaps some *reiki* could really help you work out some of those unresolved issues you're toting around with you. I sense that you've really fallen out with your spirit guide—"

"Maybe another time," I replied quickly. "What I need to know is—"

"Hist!" Vera said, cocking her head to one side.

At that very moment someone knocked on the door. Serenely, Vera opened it to reveal two respectable-looking ladies in the late stages of middle age. Both were attired in pantsuits; both had coiffed bouffants and the look of women who had worked hard all their lives. These were women who had put in time on factory lines, volunteered in church and fire-hall kitchens, all the while raising kids and keeping house. They looked as if they had just come from a shopping expedition up to the outlets. They were as incongruous at the Lock and Load as I would have been at a meeting of Historical Daughters of Santimoke County.

"Are you the Elvis people?" one of them asked pleasantly.

"Yes, we are," Vera assured them. "Please come on in."

"We're from the First Church of Elvis over to Slaughter's Crossroads," the elder of the two explained. "And what we want is to register our tribute artist in the contest."

"Of course!" Vera said graciously. From somewhere she produced some forms and gestured them to be seated at the Formica table. "You'll be entering how many artists?" she asked.

The smaller lady began printing out stuff on the form in neat, precise handwriting. "Just one." She sighed.

"You see, we had another, but he passed over," her friend added.

"Newton *was* Elvis. He was just so good, you would think that the King was right there in front of you, up on the altar of the church," her companion remarked dolefully. "When he sang 'Just a Closer Walk' in his sequined suit, why, you'd think Elvis himself was up there. Newt really had the call. It was very sad, really, the way he was taken from us."

"A tragedy. And just like the real Elvis, it was so unexpected."

"What happened?" Vera asked sympathetically.

The larger lady shook her head. "Last Christmas, when we had our church's Living Elvis Nativity down

to Route 50 by Glack's Good Oil and Propane, Newton was playing the Good Shepherd of Graceland, just
like he always did. He was wonderful at it too. Just
wonderful. He really had a feel for those Nativity moments Elvis loved so much.

"Unfortunately, one of the donkeys got loose and
ran across the highway. Newton being the kind of
man he was, well, he never hesitated. He chased that
donkey right across four lanes of traffic.

"He never even saw that car coming, did he, Hattie?"

"Never did, Millie," Hattie agreed. "The Good
Shepherd of Graceland met his tragic end in the grille
of a Lincoln Town Car."

"There was blood and sequins all over the highway," Millie said. "The rescue squad said they'd
never seen such a mess. And of course the driver of
the car was just horrified. Horrified.

"He was from the Romanian embassy in Washington. He was a big Elvis fan. Big fan. Cried like a
baby, he did. 'I keeled El-vees! I keeled El-vees!' he
kept saying, but it wasn't his fault. Newton never
looked to the right or the left, he just did what he
thought Elvis would have done, right up to the end."

"He's in that heavenly Graceland now," Millie
observed piously, with a look toward the water-
stained ceiling tiles. "There wannit a dry eye on the
rescue squad neither. His last words were, 'I done
what I come to do.' "

We all paused for a moment of silent contemplation of the late Newton, in his Good Shepherd of Graceland Elvis suit, running across four lanes of traffic to rescue a runaway donkey.

It's like the Song says. I seen the Elvis Nativity wreck on the highway, but I didn't hear nobody pray.

Vera ran her hands over her hair and shook them out at her sides again. This seemed to be her answer to any possible unpleasantness, even a Nativity tragedy.

"That's why we're entering Shelvis," Hattie explained, standing back to allow us a full view of a diminutive figure in a white fringed jumpsuit decorated with spangled hearts stepping in the doorway.

"How d'you do?" this apparition asked, stepping into the room and adjusting its aviator glasses.

"Shelvis?" I asked.

"Yes. She-Elvis. It was her idea, you know, to become a female Elvis. She got the call and the church prayed on it, and we agreed that Newton would want us to go on."

"That's right," said Shelvis, running a hand over her blue-black pompadour.

"Besides," Hattie added firmly, handing the form to Vera, "Shelvis is the best Elvis tribute artist, male, female, living or dead, you're gonna see in the Chesapeake Chapter."

"Venus Tutweiler, is that you behind that wig and those shades?" I peered at the latest Elvis curiously.

"Holly Ball? Hey, how you doin'?" Venus asked me cheerfully as she shook my hand in a grip made ironlike from her job at Patamoke Seafood. "Haven't seen you in ages!"

"You're She-Elvis?" I asked. "Venus, I never knew! Still working nights over to the seafood plant in Oysterback?"

"Still drivin' the forklift. And you?"

"Still with the *Gazette*. Boy, you look really different as Elvis," I said admiringly. "I never would have recognized you!"

"Is there something wrong with a woman bein' Elvis?" Millie challenged us.

"Elvis knows no race and no gender," Vera said gently, taking the form. "Elvis is everyone."

"Amen," Venus replied, adjusting her shades and giving us a karate pose.

"The church will be so pleased." Hattie shook Vera's hand. "We'll see you there, on Elvis's birthday!" Once again she rolled her eyes piously toward the ceiling.

"Some fun, huh?" Venus asked me with a wink. I was about to tell her that this was old home week, that another graduate of Watertown High School was also working the Lock and Load, but Venus did a couple of King-style karate moves and took off. "Savin' it for the contest, Holly!" she called over her shoulder.

After Vera had shown the ladies to the door, she turned and smiled at me. "Bang Bang would have been so pleased at the response this is getting. Elvis was his great passion in life, you know. He lived for Elvis. Elvis was his obsession.''

''And you're carrying on his work,'' I observed. ''What a wonderful tribute to his memory.''

''Well, Elvis really brought Bang Bang and I together.'' Vera smiled, throwing herself wearily into the chair vacated by Millie. A cloud of purple shawls and scarves rose up around her as she crossed her Birkenstocks on the edge of the bed.

''You mean you were interested in Elvis too?''

Vera shook her head. ''Oh, no. I didn't even know who Elvis was until I started to channel him. Now he's like my best friend and adviser. That's how I met Bang Bang. Elvis told me I had to help him out, raise his consciousness. You see, Elvis is my spirit guide.''

8

DON'T BE CRUEL

♪♪ MEMO TO ME: *RESIGN AS GENERAL MAN-
ager* of the universe.

People can get along just fine without
my meddling.

I staggered out of Albie's room just as Tonto
Shively was shuffling in, still wearing his white rubber boots. As anyone who has ever attended a Shore
muskrat-and-scrapple dinner knows, Tonto is the Waterman Elvis.

"Yippee! I been waitin' for a chance like this since
I took up Elvisin'!" he informed me gleefully.

I managed a grim grin. It was a wonder no other
waterman had drowned him after hearing his rendi-
tion of "Mama Loved the Roses" come blasting out
of the CB at 5:00 A.M. on a muggy August morning.

The way in which he serenaded his fellow crabbers was legendary in these parts. I've seen Tonto's act at the Santimoke County Watermen's Association annual banquet. Comedy is not pretty, and come to think on it, neither is Tonto.

I was standing in the parking lot, adding *Elvising— a verb like journaling?* to my notes when I heard my name being called. I looked up to see Snow White hissing at me from behind her chained-up door.

"Ssss! Ssss!" She beckoned me over.

"Jeez, Snow," I grumbled. "I'm not the vice squad." But I went anyway.

Before I could protest, the door opened and Snow dragged me inside, slamming the door behind me as if all the hounds of hell were at my back, which maybe they were.

"What the pluperfect hell?" I demanded, pulling the tail of my jacket out of the door.

Snow's eyes were ringed with mascara, and her hands were shaking as she thrust a pack of cigarettes at me. "Have one and shut up a minute," she commanded. "Tonto's so cheap, he thinks he can come out here and kill two birds with one stone."

"Or stone two birds with one kill," I said sourly, nodding at the alleged drug paraphernalia—a Baggie and a bong—out on the Formica table. Looked like she and Tonto had their own little party, I thought sourly.

"Have a Marlboro and shut up." Snow disappeared into the bathroom, and after due consideration I lit up a legal.

Damn, that 'Boro tasted good, and with no ghosts to nag me, I inhaled deeply and gratefully while my classmate tidied herself up.

While Snow splashed water I watched the finest broadcast media has to offer: several unsavory-looking people bitch-slapping each other in front of a cheering audience. At least I guessed they were cheering; the sound on the TV was off. Since I don't get to watch much daytime TV, the talk show as blood sport is something new to me. My fellow humans. Good Lord.

When Snow came back she was walking with a nervous step, her hands jerking in rhythm to some song only she could hear. She paced the floor, now peering out from behind the polyester curtains into the empty parking lot, now leaning down to pick invisible lint from the sad wall-to-wall carpet, the color of a dead pink flamingo. Her toes and her fingers were painted a hideous brilliant blue, and her hair was dreadfully dreaded.

And she was about as high as she could be.

I smoked and watched her, half afraid and half fascinated. I wanted to feel sorry for her, but I felt too much like an unindicted conspirator with my (so far legal, but watch this space) nicotine problem.

Instead, I watched her straighten the bedclothes and smooth out the pillows, fool with the picture frames, and babble on and on senselessly. "I mean, you know, you just gotta, you know, like, do it. I'm gonna get it together, you know, because I have talent, and I'm a good musician, and you know——"

Rock-star ramble, verbal diarrhea, lapsed synapses misfiring in the brain or something—but that didn't mean I had to sit here and listen to her patter. I resented Snow's whole life at that moment and resented the self-occupation that had led her to this and resented being dragged into it. I felt sick and weary. I had the option to go, so I took it.

"Well, I'll talk to ya later, Snow," I said, rising to leave and dreading the pleas to please stay that would come in a torrent. No one hates being alone so much as someone who wants an audience to witness their demons destroy them.

"Hey, whatcha hurry? Have 'nother cigarette; you wanna packa peaner butta crackers or a soda or somethin'? Man, I think you just want my cigarettes, that's all I think you want. Come on, finish up watchin' Springer with me, okay? Wassa matter? You think you're too good for me, doncha?" Snow danced around me, her whole body jerking as she sang snatches of some whining tune.

"What I think is that I have a deadline to meet," I lied, as I edged my way to the door. Snow, sensing that she was losing her audience, got right up into my space. She smelled of cigarettes and musk perfume. I didn't like her in my personal space.

"Just a cracker, huh?" she begged me. "Come on, you don't gotta go nowhere; you know you wanna stay and have another cigarette. Don't leave me alone; I have another client comin' in fifteen minutes, then you can leave, okay?" Snow pleaded with me. "I don't wanna be by myself. They might get me, you know what I mean?"

"Nobody's gonna get you, Snow, that's the doper paranoia talking," I explained as I pushed my notebook back into my bag and eased my way, inch by inch, toward the door.

But Snow wanted company. She grabbed my arm. "Come on, stay till he gets here, then I'll be okay, okay, you know what I mean? It's just that those Elvis people, ya know? They wanna get me. They know that I know stuff, you know? Stuff they don't want anyone else to know. About that Bang Bang guy."

"Well, you need to tell all that to the police," I said. All I wanted to do was get out of there; I couldn't breathe with a needy human being so far up in my face. Loner that I am, Snow's clinging was making me extremely anxious. "Yeah, yeah, whatever," I mumbled, working to get the chain bolt to open while she hovered inches from me, yammering all the while.

And she wouldn't let go of me; those iridescent blue nails were digging into my arm while her mouth was working a mile a minute. I could feel those nails through several layers of cloth. Her grip was surprisingly strong. Strong enough to strangle? The thought scared me.

"I ain't telling nothin' to no cops," she spat. "You think I'm gonna mess with the pigs? Listen, Hollis, I know, you know what I saw, and they know I know what I saw. Somebody killed that man—"

"Why didn't you tell Friendly?" I asked suspiciously.

"I told you! I don't need to deal with no pigs," Snow hissed at me. "I mean, ya know, I mean you know, he don't owe me nothin', how do I know—"

"What do you know, Snow?" I asked.

Her face closed up, and she glared at me sullenly. "What will you pay me to find out? It's worth money," she stated flatly.

"I don't pay for stories. If you want to tell me something, tell me."

She twirled a dreadlock around her finger. "I ain't talkin' unless someone gives me some money. Talk ain't cheap, ya know."

I had the feeling that she was jerking me, just to keep me in the room. She knew exactly jack shit, I decided. "Okay, okay, whatever." I made a great show of looking at my watch. "Gee, look at the time! I gotta run. I'll talk to you later, Snow."

When you're clean and sober, Snow, I thought, with only the smallest twinge of guilt as I ran to my car and left the Lock and Load Loonies to their own devices.

There is only so much you can handle when you're dealing with wack jobs, and you can't handle anymore. Everyone knows their limit; most of us just find a way to go over it, in the dim expectation that someway, somehow, people will act better eventually.

But they never do.

ON THE WAY BACK INTO WATERTOWN, I HAD TIME TO listen to Ella Fitzgerald singing Cole Porter and to think. True, I can never run for office, because I inhaled, and then some. But when it comes to crack and smack, even I have to draw a line. As Sam used to say, "The problem with doing drugs is that you end up dealing with people you'd rather not get high with."

I almost started missing him then, but I stopped that thought before it could form. I got along fine without Sam before he started haunting me, and I could get along without him now. He could sulk all he wanted to, and I couldn't care less.

Still, I would have loved to have his take on Mrs. Vera Devine. Sam would have had a lot to say about her, I knew, and for a moment I yearned for him to pick it all over with. But just for a moment. I quickly reminded myself that I was enjoying not being spooked by Sam's ghostly attentions and that I had gotten along fine without his presence, dead or alive, for years.

That was the moment my cell phone rang.

"Hollis?" Friendly's voice crackled over the line. "Where are you?"

"On my way to the paper. What's up?"

"You'd better go up to Circuit. We just got word that Appeals will reverse Judge Carroll's capital sentence on Shaw."

I sucked in my breath. "What the pluperfect hell? Shaw killed two innocent people with a Weed Eater! The jury voted him the death penalty!"

"Well, that's the fine folks on Appeals for you. They nearly always overturn capital crimes. Political correctness has turned Stalinist on us when no one was looking."

I am not a big fan of capital punishment, but on the other hand, death by lethal injection was one hell of a lot easier than being vivisected with a weed whacker. For once Friendly and I were in agreement on a political issue.

"By the way," he added casually, "the medical examiner's report just came back on Bang Bang. It's definitely a homicide. He was strangled with that red Elvis scarf around his neck. But get this: He was so full of pills that he rattled when they put him down on the metal table."

"Whoa, Friendly. What are you sayin' here?" I demanded.

"It looks like someone killed Bang Bang Devine, but he was well on his way to killing himself with all his pills. The man was stuffed like a stoner turkey with prescription drugs.''

''So what killed him, the scarf or the pills?''

''Oh, he was definitely strangled. The question is, who wrapped that long red scarf around his neck and pulled tight?'' Friendly sighed.

''You think it's Albie?'' I demanded.

''You know damned well I can't comment on that. Hell, it could have been anyone in that dump. Could have been your pal Ms. White. Could have been anyone with a beef against the Bangster. The man had lots of folks who didn't wish him well.''

''He was probably done in by those who hated Elvis impersonators,'' I suggested. ''No jury would return a guilty on that one.'' I turned off Route 50 and headed into town. A nasty thought began to form. ''Why are you telling me this now, Friendly?'' I asked.

''What? What? We're breakin' up. I can't hear you!'' he said and disconnected.

How convenient, I thought, and considered heading back to the Lock and Load. If I got there before he did, maybe I could warn Albie that he was about to become a prime-time suspect.

But if I did that I'd miss the scoop on Appeals reversing the sentence on Shaw, not to mention Frank's tight-lipped no-comment and his off-the-record take on the situation. No judge likes his decisions reversed. And that was a story I had to cover before the paper was made up. I kept on course for the courthouse.

Ormand Friendly is an evil genius.

9

LOOKING FOR
TROUBLE

♪ ♪ "IF YOU'VE GOT THAT SON OF A BITCH AL-
bie Lydekker in tow, don't put yourself
through the door," my cousin Toby Russell greeted me.

"Nice to see you too," I said as I took a stool in
the deserted bar. Down at Toby's Bar and Grill on
Beddoe's Island, he serves the living and the dead,
but he doesn't serve unpleasant people. The sign over
the back bar says so. "I guess after whatever happened last Tuesday, Albie's on the unpleasant list?" I
asked.

Toby picked up his shucking knife and resumed
work on a pile of oysters. With short, quick movements he dug the flat-bladed knife around the hinge of
the shell. With a flip of his wrist, he opened it to

expose the oyster inside. Using the edge of his blade, he scraped the succulent bivalve into a cast-iron skillet, where it joined its brethren in a sea of oyster liquor and chunks of butter.

"That goddamned redheaded peckerwood's banned for life—" he started to say, then just shook his head. "Dammit, Hollis, why'n hell do you stick up for him?"

I fished myself a Diet Pepsi out of the cooler. "I owe him that much, Toby. You know what he did for me."

"Well, you're welcome here, but he's not," my cousin pronounced grudgingly, and I didn't press my luck. When you stand well over six feet, carry two hundred sixty pounds of muscle, and look so fierce that you've had offers from professional wrestling, not too many unpleasant people mess with you after the first time.

Toby was in fine midwinter form; his hair and beard were fully grown in, giving him the aspect of an unhappy and possibly dangerous grizzly bear. All you could see were his eyes.

A lot of bad stuff happened to Toby in Vietnam that he doesn't talk about, but he and I are best friends. As the family black sheep, we have to stick together. So I knew that he wouldn't kick me out. Unlike the Horny Mallard in Watertown, Toby's— like its island clientele—is a decidedly downscale establishment, done up in Early Pool Table and Late

Stuffed Waterfowl. I also noted an Elvis poster taped to the back bar mirror and knew the thin end of the wedge of forgiveness had been inserted.

Toby noticed my gaze and shrugged. ''Well, it's for charity,'' he muttered. ''Besides, you wouldn't believe all the people who are signing up. I had no idea there were so many Elvis fans around here.''

I took a long sip of my Pepsi. ''Albie's in trouble, I think. Remember that guy they found dead at the Lock and Load? Turned out to be a homicide.''

''And the red-haired goon is involved,'' Toby said without surprise. ''Gee, how'd I know that?'' He opened another oyster.

''Don't be sarcastic, Toby, this could be serious stuff. The dead guy was Bang Bang Devine. Albie was working for him.''

''I read the paper.'' Toby turned the heat on beneath the cast-iron skillet, and slowly, the salty smell of oyster began to fill the room. The aroma made my mouth water. ''I know all about the gambling connection. Man, I wouldn't mind putting some slot machines in here. I couldn't get a lottery machine; they gave it to Miss Rose, down to the Island Light Store. Not that I wanted it—too much like work—but still . . .'' As the edges of the oysters began to curl in their liquor, Toby gently added a little half and half. He added more chunks of butter, then ground pepper over the mixture. ''So I guess it ain't gonna happen.''

I sighed. "By the way, have you seen Sam? Not that I'm curious or anything," I added quickly.

"Haven't seen hide nor hair of him or any other ghosts for quite a while," Toby said. "Except for—"

Just at that moment Friendly came swinging through the door. When he saw the expression on my face, he hesitated for a moment, but only a moment. "Don't look at me like that! I was just doin' my job!" he exclaimed warily.

"That was some trick you pulled on me! Just to keep me away from Albie! I should have known that Shaw's lawyer was just filing a routine brief, and that it would take Appeals months to hear the case—" I started, but he flung his hands up in the air.

"Paybacks are hell," Friendly admitted, ducking his head away from me. "Hey, Toby."

"Hey," Toby replied, adding more half and half and a pinch of sea salt to the pan. The oysters were almost, but not quite, simmering in the liquor and broth. Fragrant clouds of steam rose from the pan.

I watched sullenly as Friendly pulled himself a draft and took a long swallow. "Is that oyster stew?" he asked Toby, leaning over his shoulder.

"None other," my cousin replied.

"Man, this is good weather for it. I think we're gonna get some frost tonight. It's turning cold and nasty out there."

It's about to turn cold and nasty in here, I thought, but wisely, for once, I kept my mouth shut and waited. I could tell by the way Friendly was avoiding looking at me that the news was not going to be good. Whenever he tap-dances around an issue, I know there's trouble.

With a gusty sigh, Cop Boy settled himself on a barstool and took a good hit from his beer. "I had everything I could do," he started, "not to allow that witchy woman or whatever she is to read my aura. Whoo!" He shook his head. "She's *different,* hon!"

He loosened the knot in his hand-painted hula-girl tie. The man dresses like he buys his clothes at yard sales, but what am I gonna do about that?

"So what happened?" Toby asked with interest. Nosiness is a genetic trait in my family. My cousin pretends to detest gossip, but situated as he is, he can't help but know almost everything about everyone in the county, often before they do.

"We're absolutely certain that Bang Bang was done in with the scarf; the medical examiner's office has ruled it a homicide for sure. I'll spare you the gory details, but it did the job. Word is, the man's brain was like Swiss cheese; he ate those damn pills like they were candy. I guess he was imitating his idol Elvis or something."

"Ain't that awful." Toby tsked. "It said in the paper that he was settin' on the terlet too. It seems like a man ought to be safe in his own bathroom, making his own bidness."

"Or it was made to look that way," Friendly offered. "God, his wife, Vera? There's a wack job. What a piece of work. But she's got an alibi, says she was in Baltimore at a women's running-with-the-wolves group, whatever that is. She says there were a hundred women there, so someone must have seen her. Harve's checking it out." He took another sip of his beer. "Albie, on the other hand, doesn't have much of an alibi for the approximate T.O.D." He gave me a sharp look, as if I was going to say something, which maybe I was, but I decided not to. "He says he *thinks* he was in Marsh Ferry that night at a cockfight, except he can't remember anyone else who was there, or even where he was. He just started asking around town for a game, any game, and he got driven to a cockfight somewhere in the countryside. But it was dark and he didn't know where it was." Friendly sighed. "What a mess."

"Well, you don't always know who you're cocking with. You go and you start asking around for a game and that's how it goes," Toby pointed out. I wondered how he knew.

"Apparently, he lost a bundle of money," Friendly said.

"If there's a game in town, he'll be there." I sighed. "But it's a big jump from bein' a compulsive gambler to bein' a murderer. Besides, Albie's not a killer; he's run from more fights than the Italian army. He couldn't have done that. I know Albie. He'll lie, cheat, and steal, but he draws the line at murder. I know he didn't do it.''

''Yeah, hon, but he was into Bang Bang for a lot of money. Ten big ones, plus the vigorish, which grows daily at twenty percent.'' Friendly shook a cigarette from the pack and lit it. ''And his room at the Lock and Load was right next to Bang Bang's.''

''Damn.'' Toby whistled thoughtfully.

''I don't care,'' I said loyally. ''I know it was someone else.''

''Yeah, some disgruntled Elvis hater who went postal.'' Friendly looked at me through narrowed eyes. ''And there's also your pal Snow White. She coulda offed Bang Bang if he did her on the blow job.''

''Snow? She's no pal of mine. I don't think she could get it together to kill someone. She's really strung out.''

Friendly shrugged. ''Well, we've got a whole bunch of folks in Baltimore who wanted Bang Bang for one reason or another. And a lot of people around here have definite ideas about a two-bit punk opening a gambling casino in Santimoke County. I'm still interviewing people about that.''

''I went to the meeting where he proposed the casino. There were a lotta people for it. It'd bring money into the county. I wouldn't mind having some slots in here, if they paid me enough. It'd be good for bidness. I dunno about a casino though. But there were a lotta people against it too," Toby remarked. "People have a whole lotta ideas about something like that, especially the hard-shell church people and the fire departments. They're worried about competition with their bingo nights and bull roasts."

"All I know is, Bang Bang Devine is dead, and it doesn't look like anyone, even the Widow Devine, is too upset about it. Boy, is she a piece of work." Friendly took a deep swallow of his beer. "Lord, Lord, Lord." He let his breath out in a long, gusty sigh.

"Very New Age," I explained to Toby. "Lots of crystals and herbs and stuff. Not what you would expect from a Mrs. Bang Bang at all."

"Not hardly like those people from California who bought the old Gersen place down the road from your folks and turned it into a bed and breakfast?" Toby asked. "The ones who were chasing Uncle Perk around with those funny needles and stuff after his bad back?"

"Acupuncture. They wanted him to try acupuncture. It's an old Chinese medicine. And his back *does* feel better." I laughed. "But he still doesn't want to eat the tofu burgers they made for him. Yeah, Vera Devine is something like that, only more so. She says she channels Elvis. His spirit speaks through her."

Friendly did a spit take, and beer splattered all over his shirtfront. "She channels Elvis?" he asked. "You mean like one of those trance mediums?"

I nodded.

Toby shrugged. "So that's the love connection between her and Bang Bang. The man did love his Elvis."

"Marriages have been based on stranger things," I offered. "Believe me, I know."

While Friendly filled Toby in on the gory details of Vera Devine, I took out my trusty reporter's notebook and scanned through my scrawl. As usual a lot of it was illegible, but I have a good memory.

I waited for a lull in the conversation, then importantly cleared my throat.

"While I was at the courthouse on a wild-goose chase—thanks a lot, Friendly, no comment all around—I decided I may as well go past the clerk of court's office and check out the property deeds on the Lock and Load. Then I checked their business license. Both are registered to the lovely and talented Rolley Shallcross, A.K.A. Elvis Man, at a post-office box in Watertown. No Rolley Shallcross in the local phone book, and the Lock and Load number rings and rings without an answer. The friendly folk at the P.O. don't have any other information available, except that Rolley comes in periodically and checks the box." I gave them both my best aren't-I-clever look. "He's a character, and his parents left him a house and money in a conservatorship trust that just happens to be handled by a friend of mine at the bank who's his first cousin. I called Terri, and she couldn't tell me anything because of confidentiality rules, but she says she just pays his bills and gives him walking-around money. She didn't know that he managed the Lock and Load, and she questioned whether or not that's one of his fantasies. He seems to lead a life rich in delusions.''

''Elvis Man? That nut managing the Lock and Load? That's a good one,'' Toby said. As the stew began to simmer, he stirred it gently with a wooden spoon. ''Elvis Man's harmless; he's been around since I was a boy. He's not violent, he just thinks he's Elvis.''

''Pray continue,'' Friendly invited me dryly.

''So I went and looked in the files for anything relating to Rolley Shallcross. I came up empty in the criminal dockets, but I found a whole long list of housing violations in connection with the Lock and Load, which didn't surprise me one bit, since I was able to cross-reference them with the microfiches in the *Gazette*'s morgue. Apparently, there's been a long, sad string of code infractions out there, which is probably what you'd expect from an old motel that's gone S.R.O.'' I produced photocopied clips, spreading them out on the bar. ''The Baltimore lawyer who represented the case is another story entirely.'' I produced more clips, pointing to a grainy AP photo of an oily middle-aged man hustling out of a big civic building on the Western Shore. ''Remember Zap Gadsen? The lawyer who fell off his sailboat and drowned couple years back, and they never found him? The one who was almost disbarred for ethics violations a few years ago, remember? He supposedly paid off a couple of witnesses in that Holland Court failed-savings-and-loan trial, but he fell overboard before they could charge him with anything.''

''Well, that eliminates him as a suspect,'' Toby said, looking at the photo. ''I recall that story. Guy never was found, was he?''

''Gadsen is no major loss. Another courthouse barnacle comes unglued and floats downstream. *Tant pis.* Incidentally, the last housing-code violation at the Lock and Load was two years ago. No heat or hot water. Nice, for the middle of winter.'' I scanned my notes and spread out more photocopies, one of them featuring a shot of Zap Gadsen coming out of the Santimoke County Courthouse. A bleary-eyed man with an enormous pouf of greasy hair glared at the camera. ''And Terri says Elvis Man, Rolley Shallcross, was down at the state hospital in Cambridge for one of his little stays two years ago. From time to time he goes off his meds and she has to check him in to get him stabilized again. But here's Zap Gadsen in Santimoke district court, right before he fell off the boat.'' We all looked at a grainy photocopy of a grumpy-looking man, still sporting his trademark pouf, although it had started to gray a little. ''He testified the Lock and Load was fully up to code.''

''Definitely ready for a feature in *House and Gar-*

den," my cop boyfriend opined sarcastically. He shook his head. "I recall Zap Gadsen's disappearance. Went sailing all alone and never came back. They found the boat adrift near Love Point, but the body never turned up."

"Then"—I cleared my throat—"I checked Rolley Shallcross in the Baltimore directories. Then Baltimore County, then all the other Maryland counties, and finally, on the Internet. No hits there until—"

"Until?" Ormand Friendly scooped up a handful of crackers and chewed them thoughtfully. The only way I could tell he was interested was by the way his eyebrows went up into his hairline every time I mentioned a new fact.

"I went to Elvis—specifically, Elvis impersonators. Finding Elvii on the Web is a whole different ballgame. There are Elvii everywhere, in every walk of life. More Elvii than you ever dreamed existed. And there's a Rolley Shallcross, who's an Elvis *collector,* not impersonator, who has a Web page of collectibles, auction, buy sell or trade. Elvis Man *is* an Elvis collector, according to Terri, and the money she doles out to him goes to buying Elvis stuff. Harmless enough, but it feeds right into this Elvis thing at the Lock and Load." I took a deep breath. "So I went back and checked the Net for Zap Gadsen. No hits. But I confirmed Zap's status as a heavy hitter. I found that out when I went into the morgue at the paper and checked out some of his old clips. Gadsen's client list

was a who's who of scumbags across the great state
of Maryland. Every sleazy developer, every corrupt-o
savings-and-loan manipulator, every legal Twilight
Zone wack job quote-en-quote businessman you can
name used Gadsen's services. Sense a connection
here, gentleman?''

"No," Friendly remarked conversationally around
the lighting of a cigarette. I inhaled secondhand
smoke gratefully.

"That's some rough trade.'' Toby peered down at
my notes, reading upside down. "Hey, that guy paved
an entire county! And that one walked away from a
murder-one charge in Howard County. These are
some ugly customers, Hollis.''

"It was almost a who's who of quasi-legal slea-
zoids and white-collar criminals,'' I agreed. "You
wouldn't want any of these boys to move into your
neighborhood.''

"Hell, I wouldn't vote *him* onto a condo board,''
Friendly observed, pointing at a name in my notes.
"Did you see him on *60 Minutes* last year?''

"These are the kind of folks Gadsen represented.
Crooks, scum bags, and the very, very tacky. When
he drowned, Gadsen had been doing a lot to push
casinos in the state ledge. And among his clients
was—*ta-da*—B and B Enterprises!'' I announced triumphantly. "Do y'all see the connection here, or do I
miss my point?''

"Lemme see that,'' Friendly commanded, and I

held up my notebook. But I'm no fool; I didn't let go of it.

He grunted, which is his way to assent. "You think Shallcross is a paper cover for someone like Bang Bang owning the Lock and Load?"

"Could be, Cop Boy. Now, get this. Among other things, Shallcross's name is on the deed for that old cannery plant down on the river in Watertown. He also has the mortage on a house called, according to my notes, Ill Wind, right here in lovely Santimoke County." I shook my head. "I've been a reporter for almost twelve years, and I've never even *heard* of him before. But I asked the county reporter, and she said he used to turn up once in a while with public-nuisance violations when he went off his meds, but that was all she knew about him. I asked Terri. Again, confidentiality. But she seemed surprised when I mentioned the canneries, like she didn't know about them. And you can forget her as a suspect, by the way. She's a real Girl Scout and honest as the day is long. Apparently, Elvis Man hasn't let the right hand know what the left hand's doing."

"Ill Wind? Innit that on Mandrake Neck, where all o' them rich folks like the Wescotts live?" Toby asked.

"Yeah, so that would place it among the stately Wayne Manors of the rich and powerful."

"Interesting," Friendly murmured. "Except this guy ain't Batman."

"He's not even Bruce Wayne, sounds like. Must be one of those new places up on the cove."

Toby placed a steaming bowl of oyster stew on the bar. "You could get hurt messin' around Albie's gambling pals," he pointed out.

I tasted a spoonful of the stew, bit into an oyster, and sensed the tangy flavor of the Bay burst on my tongue in sweet bliss. Oyster stew is the best comfort food in the world. And right about that moment I needed some comfort. "Damn, Tobe, this's good."

Toby shrugged. "No secret. I just blow off the cholesterol and use half and half. You gotta heat up your skillet, then pour in the oysters and the oyster liquor, then bit by bit you add your half and half, then your butter, let it steep on simmer for a while, then add your salt and pepper. Couldn't be easier."

"Then how come mine always tastes so bland?" I complained. I'd never tell my mother this, but Toby's oyster stew is even better than hers. And hers is the nectar of the gods.

Toby winked. "You don't have soul."

"I guess I don't." I sighed.

Friendly looked at his watch. "Well, no rest for the weary. I've got to head on back to work. Do me a favor, Hollis."

"What's that?" I asked suspiciously.

"Let me borrow your notes and clips."

"Hey, I can't do that. Go to the courthouse and do

your own research, Cop Boy.'' I clutched them against my chest.

''Come on, just overnight. I'll give them back to you tomorrow morning. But I want to run down some of your info. Double-check it. I'll return it to you as soon as I make some photocopies,'' he promised. ''Meanwhile, hon, I think you'd better stay out of this.'' He leaned over and gave me a kiss. ''And stay away from Rolley Shallcross and the Lock and Load, okay?''

Then, neat as you could ask for, he plucked my notebook out of my fingers.

''Gimme that back!'' I grabbed at him, but Friendly was too quick for me, jumping away with a grin.

''Evidence in a murder investigation. You can pick it up tomorrow.'' He suddenly frowned, draping his arm around my shoulder in the way he does when he's concerned about me, which is often. ''Hollis, you know, as case manager I can't allow you to futz around with witnesses in a homicide investigation.''

''I wasn't going to futz, as you so articulately put it, with witnesses! I've got my job to do too, you know. This is illegal. Well, maybe not illegal, but it's bad journalism,'' I concluded weakly.

''So is tampering with a murder investigation,'' he told me, dead serious now, in total cop mode. ''Hollis, this could turn nasty. You're not playing with some local yokels; the Devine guys are big boys, and they play for keeps.'' He poked a finger at me, his green eyes cold as river ice. ''Hollis, if I catch you messing in this, I swear I will arrest you for obstructing justice, because jail is the only place I know where you'll be safe. Is that clear?''

''Aw, what the pluperfect hell—'' I started, then stopped. ''You're serious, aren't you?''

''As serious as a heart attack. Stay away from Albie and from the Lock and Load,'' Friendly commanded.

I gritted my teeth and pushed my hand through my hair. Taking orders is not my forte. ''I knew this would happen sooner or later.'' I was whining and I knew it and I couldn't get that awful tone out of my voice, no matter how much I tried, and the more I tried, the more that edge penetrated my voice.

Friendly sighed. ''Don't go off half-cocked, Hollis. There are serious conflict-of-interest issues here. Not just between you and me, but between you and this story. You know you can't write about Albie objectively.''

I set my jaw mulishly. I was about to say that I sure could, when I realized that Friendly was dead-on right. Oh, how I hate when that happens. But I knew he was right. Conflict of interest was written all over this in big, bright Day-Glo neon letters a mile high. Conflict of interest between his job and my job. Conflict of interest between my personal life and my job. Conflict of interest everywhere. I felt as if I had finally joined the mainstream, where people don't seem to be concerned about that stuff.

"It would seem that Albie had a little conflict of interest going on here too. Certainly, his interests and Bang Bang's were in conflict," Toby suggested.

"You've got a little tiny conflict of interest here too, Friendly," I snapped. "You agreed to be a judge in this damned Elvis contest."

"Don't make a joke out of everything, Hollis," Friendly warned me darkly. He looked more like Harrison Ford ridden hard and put away wet than ever, and I knew he was on the edge of one of his famous ballistic tempers.

I wasn't in the mood for creative cussing. I really wasn't even in the mood for another fight with a man, dead or alive. Or a woman, or a child, or anything animal, vegetable, or mineral.

But me being me, I had to get my licks in. "You knew when you started running me what I do and who I am," I said in that damned whiny voice. "You know that I don't like being told what to do. You know that Albie's my godfather and—"

"And I sure as hell know that I don't want to see you end up with an ice pick in the ear either," Friendly finished grimly. "They don't pay you enough for that."

Well, he had me there, and I knew it. They sure don't pay me enough to die for this job. "Oh, shit," I growled and went into sulk mode, because I hate be-

ing put in the wrong, even when I know someone else
is right.

"You're out of your league on this one," Toby
advised me. "Albie's playing with some big-league
bad boys, Hollis."

"I'll call you when I have some news." Friendly
tucked my notebook into his pocket. "Sit tight, hon,
okay? Promise me?"

But he was out the door before I could protest. Or
promise.

"Dammit to hell, I did all that legwork and he just
waltzes out the door with all my information!" I
grumbled to Toby.

"Orm's right, you know," my cousin informed
me. "You don't want to mess with these people."

I moodily scraped out oyster stew from my bowl,
getting every last succulent drop. Not even a ploy
from Friendly could destroy my pleasure in hot comfort food on a cold day.

I was just about to wish that Sam was there when it
happened.

The jukebox switched itself on, and a soft, croon-
ing voice invited us to return to sender.

"Life's like that, darlin'," a deep voice full of
Mississippi molasses drawled from the shadows.

I thought the bar was empty, so I spun around,
startled.

I should have known.

The dust and murk seemed to aggregate itself into

a shape. A human shape. But it was the blue suede shoes I saw first. They weren't just blue; they were glowing with the atomic half-life of a hubba-hubba shade of bright sapphire.

"Don't step on my shoes. Whatever you do, don't step on my blue suede shoes."

My eyes rose past the shiny black pegged pants and the hot-pink sports coat richly trimmed with black piping. They stopped at the hair. The hair had a life of its own. Deep blue-black, combed and greased into great whorls and swirls that cascaded down his forehead like a waterfall. I swallowed hard.

"I-I wouldn't dream of it," I managed to whisper.

The lips—those full, sensual lips—curved into a crooked smile, the trademark sneer.

"Sorry to scare you, ma'am," the ghost—for it was, indeed, a ghost—said softly. "But I feel kinda special about these shoes."

I stared at them with grudging admiration. "I can see why," I croaked. "Are you . . . him?"

The revenant chuckled. "Let's say I'm him in spirit."

I looked around to see if he was accompanied by Bigfoot, UFO aliens, and Flukeman. Uh-uh.

"He comes around every year about this time for the oyster stew," Toby explained. "Living or dead, the man loves his oyster stew."

"When we come through here with the band back in '54, I discovered good oyster stew," the spirit remarked. "My mama loved oyster stew." The ghost sighed, and there was the sound of a thousand old bluesmen and hillbilly guitar pickers in that gust of air. "Times were different then, more innocent, closer to the bone. I'd cut a couple records for Sam Phillips in Memphis, played the Opry and Louisana Hayride, and the next thing I knew, the band and I were on the road. Billed me as the Hillbilly Cat, and Scotty and Bill were the Blue Moon Boys. There we were, playin' these one-night stands all over the South, ridin' around, singin' in no-name clubs and bars and county fairs, and sleepin' in the bus, eating at places so bad that your belly would ache for a week after, stayin' in motels when we could afford it, places so cheap you had to fight the cockroaches for a towel when you finally got a shower."

"Sounds like the Lock and Load," I breathed.

"I think we stayed at that place, and it was nasty back then too! But we were playin' the music, and that's what mattered to us. The music just gets in you and you gotta move, you gotta sing, 'cause if you don't, what have you got? They weren't payin' us more than a few dollars a night, but it was better than drivin' a truck." He grinned that twisted grin. "Besides, the girls loved it. They'd yell and scream when I started to move and jump . . . yeah! But there we were, playin' these dives all over the place, and we ended up in Maryland. I'd never been that far north before. Never been that cold, that cold to the bone. It was April, and it was still cold. Well, there we were one night in a little club, somewhere up near Cecil, and it was Easter and so cold, and we was all lonely for our families and far from home, but the lady who ran the place, she took one look at all these poor ole freezin' boys and she whupped up a big ole pot of oyster stew, which we had never had before. Now, I'm an upland country boy and used to plain food, and I tell you, those oysters were downright scary-looking, all gray and slimy. But one of the other boys in the band was from New Orleans, and he knew his oyster stew, and he made us try it. Man! I'm glad he did! After peanut-butter-and-banana sandwiches, oyster stew is the best thing y'all got up here!'' He hunkered over his bowl again.

I noted that he was inhaling the essence of a steaming bowl of Toby's best.

Toby says that we can both see ghosts because we inherited the talent from our Mum Mum Russell, who had Santimoke Indian blood. Toward the end of her long life, she also saw the Grand Army of the Potomac camped out among her Beefsteak tomatoes, but I hope and pray Toby and I don't go that far over. For some reason ghosts like Toby's Bar and Grill. It's probably his cooking. And the fact that he'll let them run a tab.

Until Sam showed up, I didn't know about this aspect of Toby's life. I guess I thought all the dead people were just extremely tired or shy or both. But now I know. Oh, do I know.

The jukebox lurched into life, and I was jolted into the present again.

Both the ghost and Toby were grinning at me.

"So," I asked conversationally, "are you Elvis, or are you a ghostly tribute artist?"

The ghost just shook his head. "Darlin', you know that E isn't dead; he's just takin' a rest from fame." From an interior pocket he withdrew a set of aviator glasses and placed them over his eyes.

That didn't answer my question, but pressing the issue seemed to be rude. I glanced at Toby, hoping for a clue, but he was busy with his glass-polishing. I tried another tack. "I guess you're Fifties' Elvis? As opposed to, like, black-leather Sixties' Comeback Elvis or Las Vegas Elvis in the spangled jumpsuit?"

"I'm the Spirit of Rock and Roll," the revenant replied, running thumb and forefinger along the sharp pleat in his pants. "Wherever there's music, Elvis lives forever, past, present, and future. I'm the fifties' incarnation. I'm like a lotta ghosts, kinda partial to that time when it was all in front of me." He chuckled pleasantly.

I thought about that for a minute, sipping my Pepsi. This was turning into a philosophical barroom discussion, the kind you have at 4:00 A.M. on some dark night of the soul. But at Toby's it's *always* 4:00 A.M.

on some dark night of the soul. No wonder haunts and watermen like this place so much.

A tiny little smile played around my new ghost pal's lips. He was amused by my puzzlement.

"So," I said, "who killed Bang Bang Devine?"

"Ah, ah, ah!" The ghost wagged a finger at me. "You know I can't tell you that."

"He don't know either," Toby sniggered.

The ghost shrugged and straightened up, looking a trifle offended. "Well, maybe I don't know *everythin'*, darlin'," he drawled, "but I can tell you this. *I* didn't do it." He and Toby laughed, as if this were the best joke in the world.

"Please tell me Albie didn't do it," I begged, but he just grinned and inhaled his oyster stew, nodding to the beat of the music.

"Don't know that either. It's all a mystery to me."

I closed my eyes and sighed. Trust a ghost to talk to you in circles and not give you any useful information.

Somewhere, I thought, there is a place where the sun is shining and the birds are singing and people aren't haunted by ghosts, editors, ne'er-do-well godfathers, and boyfriends who just happen to see you as a conflict of interest. When I find that place, I will go there. But until then I am stuck here.

"Lighten up, E, my cousin's actually sufferin' over that red-haired fool," Toby counseled.

"Oh, my," the ghost said apologetically. "I'm so

sorry. I keep forgetting how seriously y'all—the living—take everything.'' He thrust out a hand beringed in ghostly jewels. You could see the pink of his jacket through his flesh. Like most ghosts he was translucent, and when I took his hand, I almost passed through him. He felt dry and cool. "It's a pleasure to meet you, Hollis. You can just call me E, like Toby does."

"Okay, E," I agreed.

"Now," he said, adjusting his thin silver-lamé tie, "I guess you oughta get a move on, don'tcha think?"

"A move on where?"

"Why, to make up with Sam, of course. You can't have him just floating around out there, can you?"

"Look, Mr. Pres—"

"E, darlin'. Just call me E."

"Okay. E, I don't have time to look for Sam. My godfather's in real trouble and—"

The spirit cocked me a look over his shades. "If you can find Sam, you can find out who killed Bang Bang," he offered.

I was getting a headache. "How do I find Sam?" I asked in what I hoped was a reasonable tone of voice.

"You know, your fight with Sam reminds me of my original blue suede shoes. They cost me $29.99, a lot of money in those days. I lost them somewhere on the road when we was touring that summer around here, playing the county fair. They were my good-luck shoes." He held out a foot to show me his spirit shoes, as if I hadn't seen them before. They would have been hard to miss.

"You could get a real pair of original Elvis blue suedes at the tribute-artist contest," I said, pointing to the poster. "That's the first prize."

E looked thoughtful. "Thank you, thank you very much. That's interesting information. Now, let me give you something in return. You listen to the King, darlin'. You see, when you lose track of where you've been, you lose track of where you're goin'. Then you forget how to rock and roll, darlin'. That's why I'm the Spirit of Rock and Roll Past, uh-huh."

"I don't believe this," I grumbled. I was getting a bigger headache now. "How's this supposed to help me find out who killed Bang Bang?"

"Uh-huh, uh-huh," E growled, listening to a beat only he could hear. "Don't chew stomp on ma blue suede shews, uh-huh."

"Oh, boy, Zen Elvis."

E straightened his string tie and frowned at me. "Now, that would be the Ghost of Elvis Future," he informed me. "He's more postmodern than me."

"Sorry. Say, wait a minute. What do you mean, the Ghost of Elvis Future?"

"That's all right, you didn't know." E dismissed my question. "So, what do ya say? Where's your rock and roll past?"

I looked at Toby. He just shrugged. "Hey, it's your life," he said.

Well, when the King of Rock and Roll gives you advice, what do you do?

"Okay," I agreed. "I'll look for Sam. He's my rock and roll past."

E's grin was like sunshine.

"Yahoo!" he whooped.

"Now, wait a minute," I begged. "Where do I start?"

"Why, darlin', you've got to get back your rock and roll past. Uh-huh, uh-huh, huh-uh!" He gave a little pelvic wiggle. "Thank yew, thank yew very much," he said as he faded away into the shadows.

10

ARE YOU LONESOME TONIGHT?

♪ ♪ A CHILLY WIND BLEW IN FROM THE BAY. The moon, round and distant, hung in the dark blue sky just above the horizon, its light casting a scattering of dancing diamonds across the waves. A few puffy clouds blew across the night sky as if driven by witches. Far up the road I saw the lights at Mandrake Manor go off, one by one. I had no doubt if they knew I was lurking in the Wescott family graveyard, they would call the state mental hospital in Cambridge. And I would have precious little defense.

I sat in the car for a moment, wondering what I was doing here. I gazed out across the old tombstones, the urns, and the weeping willows and the brick table slabs. Very few people had the land or the means to maintain a private family graveyard these days. The illustrious Wescott dead, two hundred years of them, lay here—at least their mortal remains did. No doubt many of their souls were in climates considerably warmer than this bare January night could offer. The Wescott wealth and power had been accumulated in interesting ways and in interesting times.

Wind from the water rustling through loblolly pines is one of the saddest sounds in the world. I pulled the front of my coat together against a chill that pierced to the bone, raising my face to the starry night as I slid out of my car and made my way across the stiff brown grass. The cast-iron gate creaked on its hinges as I entered the family plot.

Sam's tombstone shone in the moonlight as only new and expensive marble can. I slipped and slid across the grass, plopped myself down and draped myself over it like the heroine of an extremely bad country-and-western song, and prepared to eat a large helping of ectoplasmic crow.

I read his name and dates, tracing them with my finger. The marble was like ice.

"Are you there, Sam?" I knocked on the stone.

I waited. The only sound I heard was the rustle of the wind in the pines and the hungry lapping of water against the beach below.

"Now I know I'm crazy, as if there had ever been any doubt," I said. "I'm sitting out here freezing to death, talking to a tombstone, and I'm not even sure if you're around here or not.''

From my pocket I took a miniature bottle of Bailey's Irish Cream and swigged. ''Oh, yeah,'' I continued, ''you were right, I was wrong, okay?''

Nothing.

I leaned against the stone, breathing into the cold, polished surface. ''I said I was wrong,'' I repeated. ''Come on, Sam. I'm—'' I choked on the words; this was killing me. ''I'm *sorry,* okay?''

Nothing.

Perhaps Sam had really cut out for the long, long trail this time. Maybe he'd finally checked out of this heartbreak hotel we call life. Maybe—I gasped out loud—he was *haunting someone else*! A stab of unexpected jealousy went through my heart.

I wrapped my coat tightly around myself against the cold. The damp ground was freezing my butt right through my jeans.

Still, I persisted in sitting there like an idiot. ''You know,'' I said to the empty air, ''you're a lot more fun as a ghost than you were when you were alive. And you have made me see things differently. The glass isn't always half empty now. I have a lot more fun now, and it's because of you.''

I was talking into the air, but I didn't care. ''Sam, when you were alive you really hurt me like nobody ever hurt me before. We were still on our honeymoon in Fort Lauderdale when you sent me to the marina store for a six-pack of soda, and while I was gone you just sailed away in the boat. I was standing there on the dock watching you motor out to sea, and I stood there for an hour, waiting for you to come back, because I thought it was a joke.'' I took another swig of Bailey's. The sweetness of it rolled on my tongue, comforting me. "Do you have any idea what it's like when you realize the man you thought you were going to spend the rest of your life with literally sails out of your life?''

Another swallow of Bailey's slid easily down my throat. "I've got issues here, Sammy boy, big issues. I can't trust anyone, and I have a history of dysfunctional relationships. I could play all the roles on a talk show, that's the kind of issues you left me with.''

I thought I heard something, but I didn't look up. I felt as if I had to keep talking, as if the truth would weave a web.

"Sam, you can be really irritating and you can get me into a lot of trouble, but your coming back has also done me a lot of good. I know you're sorry about what happened, and I know haunting me is a way of expressing all that repentance. I know you feel like you wasted your life, and the way that your life ended will tie you to earth for a long, long time until you can make amends—''

Sam sniffed. It was an unmistakable sound, and I knew it was his. I sensed him lurking in the shadows.

Sulking, no doubt. But at least he was listening to what I had to say.

I took another swig of Bailey's. "And I'm willing to forgive you. If," I added quickly, "you can forgive me."

I sensed rather than heard Sam reclining on top of his thick gray headstone. He might not be buying, but he was at least considering my sales pitch.

"I mean that, Sam," I added. "I really need you right now. Things are pretty botched up. Not just with Albie, but with Friendly."

There. I'd uttered the dreaded name, mentioned the one person Sam felt threatened by. I continued.

"I honestly have no idea where things are going with him. It's one day at a time, Sam. But I like him, and I feel pretty comfortable with him, even though we have some problems about our jobs conflicting and the way I didn't tell him everything I knew about what happened to Busbee Clinton."

More Bailey's. I saw Sam's translucent leg in the moonlight, swinging nervously along the face of his tombstone. It cast no shadow. At least he was starting to corporate. He was materializing. That was a good sign.

"Friendly's not going away, Sam," I told him firmly. "At least not for now. Maybe sometime down the road things won't work out. But this relationship means something to me. He's a decent man, maybe the first good guy I've ever been involved with." I took a deep breath. "I know this fight isn't really about Albie. It's about Friendly."

"Yeah," Sam said softly above my head.

I was encouraged. At least he was talking now.

"Sam, you're dead and I'm alive, which is one of the main obstacles to us getting back together—as a couple. It's like that old joke about a mixed marriage. 'I was human; he was Klingon'?"

Sam grunted.

I waited.

After a long while in which the wind grew colder and the moon rose into the sky, he slid off the tombstone and settled down beside me. Together we looked out across Chesapeake Bay at the distant, twinkling lights on the Bay Bridge.

Sam's hand, dry and cold, settled into mine. "Okay," he said. "Holl, I am truly and honestly sorry about what I was and what I did to you when I was alive. That's what I'm trying to make up for, now that I'm dead. Do I *have* to say all this stuff?"

"Yes."

"Oh, man, you women really know how to hurt a guy. I'm also real sorry for all the times I've driven you crazy since I became a ghost. Now can we change the subject?"

"To what?"

"Well, there's probably a good reason why Friendly wants you to stay away from the Lock and Load."

"What are you suggesting?"

"I think he wants to arrest Albie. And I'm not certain he's wrong."

"Sam! Albie didn't do it! I've got to get out there and warn Albie. But if Friendly catches me—"

"Heh, heh, heh. There's always a way. . . ."

"No, Sam! Friendly would—"

"Friendly—ha! Come on, Hollis, the game is afoot!"

11

SHAKE, RATTLE, AND ROLL

♪ ♪ IF SOMEONE HAD TOLD ME I'D BE DRIVING around the county on a subzero blue night with a ghost, I'd have told them to up their Prozac.

But there I was again, driving Mr. Sam. Not only does he dislike my choice of tapes, he is also deeply suspicious of my transportation choice. I soon had him caught up to speed on events. But it almost seemed as if he wasn't really listening.

"How can you drive around in this piece of Japanese junk?" he asked plaintively. "If I were still alive, I'd buy you a Beemer. German, that's the way to go."

"Oh, that's all right," I said quickly. "I'm pretty happy with the Civic. It runs and it doesn't go off bridges," I reminded him nastily. "As long as Cousin Larry keeps finding chopped parts at bargain rates, we're okay."

"Cousin Larry the survivalist Dittohead is definitely one of my favorite in-laws. But, hey, that adventure was fun!" Sam said defensively, shoving a Paul Robeson tape into the deck.

"Never mind. Where are we going?" I should have asked that one before we left the graveyard, but blind faith in ghosts is one of my weaknesses.

"Follow that dream," Sam replied vaguely, before lapsing into a spate of harmonizing on "Old Man River." "Elvis shoulda recorded that," he mused. "Can't believe he's hangin' around Toby's."

"If it is Elvis and not the ghost of an impersonator. Looking eternally for his lost blue suede shoes, at that." The moon was full, and the cold, pale light cast the naked countryside into sharp silhouette and shadow. The empty fields were so white and frosty it was like traveling through a lunar landscape. Darkness comes early in the dead months of winter, and everything touched with frost seemed to glow. A dreamscape with ghost on the dark side of the moon.

Anything was possible, so I drove, watching the road, a long silver strip cut from the land. Paul Robeson's voice was silenced as the tape ended.

"This is nuts," I stated flatly. "What are we doing?"

But Sam was snapping his fingers in time to some

song only he could hear. "We are gonna pay a little visit to the Lock and Load," he finally said.

Out here in the country, the blue shadows were punctuated here and there by the distant lights of farmhouses reflected in the cold clear sky, where the stars shone down in perfect crystal clarity. Moonlight cast long shadows, and things lurked out there that were alive and yet not alive, I noted as a haggard fox darted out across the road and disappeared into the woods.

"Turn here," Sam would say from time to time, or "take the left fork up here," and that was all the directions I got.

I thought I knew this county pretty well, having been born and raised here, having covered it for almost a decade for the paper, but Sam was taking me to a whole new road I didn't know existed. Granted, it was a rutted dirt lane that seemed to end in the middle of nowhere or, to be more precise, a stubbled soybean field, which is the same thing.

"Okay, where the pluperfect hell are we?" I asked in what I hoped was a reasonable tone.

"Look out over there." Sam pointed, and I followed the direction of his pointing finger. I saw some dim lights twinkling on the edge of the field and heard the distant rush of traffic.

"Route 50, dead ahead. That is the Lock and Load, and this is the back entrance, so to speak," Sam pointed out happily. "We can walk across this field here."

The next thing I knew, we were out of the car and walking over the fields. He was floating, actually, skimming along on the cold blue air just above the blunted stubble of the rutted field. When I stumbled, he took my hand. It felt like ice.

Sam laughed. "Damn, it feels good to be on the track again!"

"Aw, I missed you too," I admitted.

As we crossed the harvested fields, I noticed that I cast a long, rippling shadow, but Sam cast nothing at all. You could see the moonlight through him too.

As we drew closer, the sound of several voices raised in song echoed dimly around us, carried away on the wind. I couldn't tell for sure, but it really sounded like the Lawrence Welk people singing "Blue Suede Shoes."

The behind of the Lock and Load was even shabbier than the front. It looked like a World War I bunker. Even in moonlight the rotting cinder block was morose. Tiny bathroom windows with ripped and rusting screens provided the only openings in the blank wall. A garden of trash and litter bloomed in the weeds and neglect. Old cans and plastic bottles took on a sinister aspect, and bits of nameless dreck and garbage slowly melted into the landscape. A rat chewing a tattered plastic bag startled me with his noise, and I jumped, causing a scurrying and squeaking of invisible things better left unseen as they darted into the shadows.

"Whoa! Bad vibes!" Sam hissed.

"Saaaay," I asked suspiciously, "Vera Devine doesn't really channel Elvis, does she?"

But he had disappeared, as ghosts are wont to do when you have a couple of hard questions.

I looked around distastefully at the weeds and the trash. "Great," I grumbled. "Now what?"

A piercing scream answered that question.

Now, piercing screams may be part of the soundtrack at the Lock and Load, but I'm not generally around to hear them, especially when lurking around the back of the place. I was ready to run.

Before I could move, one of the tiny windows was flung open, and a pair of hands scrabbled at the screening. "Help me, help me," someone was choking. "Oh, God, oh, God, oh, God, I don't want to die—oh, God!"

"Snow?" I exclaimed and ran to help my old high school classmate. She was gasping and crying as she ripped away the screening with raw and bleeding fingers, trying to lift herself up to push herself through the small hole.

"Help me, help me," she begged hysterically, scrabbling to gain some kind of purchase from inside. "Oh, God, oh, God, he's trying to kill me—"

As I reached up and pulled the ancient rusting screen apart, it fell away to orange dust and sharp points that dug into my hands. I could hear someone pounding on the bathroom door behind Snow so hard that the cheap wood bent inward on its hinges as if were made from cardboard, which maybe it was.

Driven by fear, Snow scrambled up on the toilet and thrust her upper body through the window. "Oh, my God, my God, my God," she kept saying, trying to push her hips through the opening. She dangled in the air, clawing desperately at the frame of the window.

The door bent and cracked but stayed on its hinges. Even in the dim moonlight you could see it swell inward, as if a great weight had been thrown against it. I half-expected to see Jack Nicholson thrust his head through a hole, screaming, "Heeere's Johnny!"

Snow was looking right at me, but in her panic and fear she didn't really see me; she just clawed desperately at anything.

"Oh, my God, oh, my God, oh, my God, I'm stuck," she moaned.

I did what I could; I took hold of Snow's shoulders and pulled. Well, it was sort of like trying to push a fifty-pound sack of potatoes through the eye of a needle, but just as the cheap lock gave way on the door, I got a final adrenaline rush, pulled as hard as I could, and Snow popped through the window like an air bag, falling on top of me and sending us both rolling through the trash, some of which I didn't even want to think about without a latex covering on my brain.

"Oh, my God, oh, my God, oh, my God," Snow was crying, clutching me for dear life. "He's gonna kill me, he's gonna kill me!"

I managed to get to my knees, with Snow still hanging on to me like a giant killer squid, and looked up at the bathroom window. It was dark and still. No noise was coming from the bathroom, and no drooling psycho killer stuck his ugly old hockey mask outside.

"What the pluperfect hell was that all about?" I gasped, but Snow was still having what my Mum Mum Russell used to call the vapors.

"Oh, my God, oh, my God, oh, my God," she whimpered, shaking. I was trying to pry her fingers off my arms when the bathroom window next door banged open.

"What the hell is goin' on out there? Can't a man get some sleep without this whole place comin' down on him?"

Albie, of course. I felt a huge sense of relief, which maybe I shouldn't have. Albie is not much good in a crisis.

"It's Hollis, Albie! Someone tried to kill Snow! Run around front and grab him before he gets away!" I yelled while Snow gripped my torso in a hold that would have pleased Hulk Hogan.

"Huh?" Albie said. I guess he thought we were raccoons.

"Around the front! Go catch him! He tried to kill

Snow! Move, Albie!'' I hollered. "Dammit, Snow, let go of me! That hurts!''

Albie's head disappeared, and Snow rolled away from me.

Interestingly enough, no one else even peeked out their windows, and I could hear a lot of music going. I guess deafness was a survival technique at the Lock and Load.

"What happened, Snow?''

She was gulping air in huge swallows, lying on her stomach in the dreck and dead weeds. Suddenly, she started to vomit, and I rolled back and let her rip. I hadn't seen anyone throw up like that since college. Generally, I like to avoid projectile heaving whenever I can. The stench of bile, bananas, and peanut butter filled the frosty air.

"He-he tried to ch-choke me to d-d-death,'' she spat. Then she puked some more.

I waited anxiously for Albie to come back. Who knew but what the killer wasn't lurking about, coming around the back of the motel to do us both in?

I looked around for a weapon. If I wanted to re-cycle someone to death, I was in luck. Death by Sty-rofoam, soda can, or detergent bottle was definitely a possibility. I saw a longneck beer bottle in the weeds and went for it, cracking it against the cinder block. A jagged longneck makes a nice defensive weapon, I've learned over the years I've spent watching bar fights at Toby's.

So there I was, broken beer bottle in hand, waiting for a strangler, guarding a vomiting grunge tramp. Does it get any better than this?

When a big dark shadow came loping around the side of the building, I went into full defensive mode. "Aiiiieee!" I cried, like I knew karate or something. I must have picked up more Elvisness than I knew.

"Jesus H. Christ in a bandbox!" Albie screeched as I proffered the jagged edge of the bottle in his direction. "It's me!" I guess it was, but clad only in boxer shorts and an undershirt, he looked more like the Living Skeleton of Montreal.

"Did you see anyone?" I demanded. "Was there anyone out there?"

"Just an Elvis," Albie replied, looking around. "Boy, what a dump. Is she okay?" He'd finally noticed Snow. "What's wrong with her?" he asked, scratching his head. A stray ace of diamonds drifted out of his shorts.

"He t-tried to choke me!" Snow sputtered. "Elvis tried to choke me!"

Albie gave me a look like I was really clueless. "Which Elvis?"

"Why, the Elvis who came out of Snow's room, that's which Elvis!"

"The Elvis who tried to k-kill me!" Snow gasped as she gave a convulsive heave into the weeds.

"Elvis tried to kill you?" Albie asked stupidly.

For a moment I thought Sam had done it, although

it was hard to figure out how a ghost could choke someone. Ghosts are generally nonviolent, because it's hard to put a hurting on someone your hand goes right through.

"H-he tried to ch-ch-oke me with a p-peanut-butter-and-banana sandwich!" Snow whimpered.

"Huh?" Maybe I really was clueless.

"H-he tried to s-stuff it down my th-throat!"

"Elvis tried to kill you with a peanut-butter-and-banana sandwich?" Albie repeated dimly. It occurred to me that my godfather was so dumb that if you locked him in a grocery store, he'd starve to death.

Snow nodded miserably. "I've never been so scared in m-my life!" She wiped her mouth on her Big Pecker's Bar and Grill T-shirt. "I was settin' there watchin' *Melrose Place* when somebody knocks onna door. So I open it and this Elvis pushes past me, grabs me, throws me on the bed, and tries to stuff this sandwich down my throat—" She gagged again, and Albie and I jumped back to avoid being splattered.

"Peanut-butter-and-banana   sandwiches   were Elvis's favorite food," Albie announced thoughtfully. "Maybe the guy had the wrong room."

"Well, did you see where he went?" I was yelling, but I didn't care.

"Who?" Albie asked.

"One of the Elvii!" I was ready to smack him, her, or both of them. "The person who just tried to kill Snow!"

Albie scratched himself. "My Elvii wouldn't kill anyone," he protested loyally. "But I did see one comin' outta her room when I come back here."

"That man tried to kill her!" I yelled.

Albie squinted at Snow, who was not much to look at, even at the best of times. "Somebody tried to kill *her*?" he asked dubiously.

"No, Albie. Snow and I just enjoy hanging around the back of this dump, screaming," I replied nastily. "How could you let him get away? Don't you know the cops think *you* killed Bang Bang?"

"Well, yeah, but—huh? Me?" He didn't seem terribly upset by it.

"What's goin' on back here?"

"Yeah, can't a person get some rehearsal time around here?"

"You're interruptin' my solo!"

Suddenly, Elvii began to appear from everywhere. Short Elvii, tall Elvii, fat Elvii, skinny Elvii, white Elvii, black Elvii, even green Elvii. They all converged out of the darkness, their sequins glittering and rhinestones sparkling, their thick black ducktails and aviator shades dim and ghostly in the moonlight. "What the hell's goin' on back here, Albie?" a jumbo-size Elvis in a red sateen jumpsuit asked.

"Yeah, for sure. First you book us into this dump, now you got people screamin' and yellin' and carryin' on and it ain't us!" A tiny Elvis in purple sequins, who sounded like Venus Tutweiler, grumbled. "Hey, Hollis," she added without surprise.

Snow, not unnaturally, squealed in horror as more and more Elvii converged on the scene.

"Are all these people staying here?" I asked, dismayed.

"Well, yeah," Albie agreed. "This here is the Chesapeake Chapter of the Elvis Tribute Artist Society. They're all gathered here for the show. They were rehearsin' in the lounge. This is Holly Ball, Elvii; she's a judge in the contest."

"Which one of them tried to hurt you, Snow?" I demanded.

Someone handed her a flashlight, and she slowly scanned the faces. Elvii all, and they all looked, if not innocent, not really guilty either. They just looked like a pack of Elvis impersonators who were as in the dark as I was. Except for one guy in a white ice-cream suit, string tie, and fedora.

"What Elvis are you supposed to be?" I asked curiously.

The man took the cigar out of his mouth and politely tipped his fedora. "Oh, I'm a Colonel Parker impersonator," he told me cheerfully.

Snow shook her head. "I-I can't tell," she whined uncertainly. "They all look alike!" she wailed.

Snow had a point. How could you tell one Elvis from the other? Behind the wigs and the shades and the costumes, they all looked the same—like Elvis—

especially if you didn't have a chance to get a good look at Killer Elvis before he shoved a sandwich down your throat. Interchangeable Elvii, the perfect disguise. Anyone or anything could be under those wigs and shades. I wasn't entirely certain one of them wasn't E.

"Albie, what's goin' on out there? Come back to bed!" From the bathroom window of my godfather's palatial room at the Lock and Load, Vera Devine, wearing something very sheer and translucent, peered out the window. Evidently, her mourning period for the late great Bang Bang was over, since she had obviously found consolation in the arms of Big Red.

"Good Lord, Albie," I hissed, "couldn't you all wait until the corpse was cold?"

My godfather had the grace to look slightly abashed. "In a minute, Vera, my karma noodle," he told her.

"I'm getting cold in here, Albie," she crooned. "My *chakras* are losing fire." With a little frisson that set her ample boobs a-bobbing, she closed the window.

"Oh, Albie," I said, totally disgusted.

"Can't we talk about this later?" he asked me sotto voce. "It looks bad in front of the tribute artists."

"One of whom tried to kill Snow," I pointed out. "Jesus, Albie, what is this, *The Attack of the Killer Elvii*?"

Someone must have finally gotten disgusted enough to call 911. Somewhere on Route 50, the wail of sirens rose and fell on the frigid air, and from the Dippy Donut next door, interested patrons, including a couple of county deputies, were congregating to gawk from the safety of the parking lot.

"Oh, jeez, the cops," I muttered. "Great. Now *I'm* gonna get arrested. Albie, Friendly's coming to haul you in for questioning! That's why I came here! To warn you!"

Albie frowned and stuck out his chin. "Let 'em arrest me! I didn't kill Bang Bang, and I'll tell 'em so too!"

"Well, Friendly thinks you did, and he's on his way!"

"I don't need no cops." Snow shivered. "I've got a stack of F.T.A.'s. I'll end up in jail tonight!" She turned to me and clung to my arm, once again doing her limpet act. "Hollis, get me outta here! Someone's tryin' to kill me!"

"We don't need this kinda P.R.," Albie agreed. In spite of the frigid air, he was sweating. "Get her outta here, Hollis, please," he whispered. "All I need is some crack whore makin' trouble, and this whole thing is over and done with. I gotta pay off that ten grand or else!"

"You seem to be doing a good job of paying it off right now," I snarled, jerking my head in the direction of his room, where at this point Vera was probably adjusting her personal *fêng shui* in anticipation of Albie's *chai.*

"Aw, Hollis, don't be like that," Albie begged me. "Please, just help me out just this one time. Get her outta here; we don't need any more trouble! Vera'll kill me! She'll put a curse on me or somethin'!"

"Say, Hollis." An Elvis in a black cape with fangs spoke up, in a voice that sounded like it belonged to Big Tuna Scroggins, Drac-Elvis. "What's goin' on here? We need our sleep, ya know. Elvisin' is hard work!"

There were agreeing grumbles all around. In the dark, behind a cheesy motel on Route 50, a pack of disgruntled Elvis impersonators can look rather threatening. Or at least rather surreal.

The sirens were getting closer. I thought about Friendly's threat to jail me for obstructing justice, and I knew he was prepared to carry through with it. The women's section of the Santimoke County Detention Center made the Lock and Load look like the Laura Ashley Suite at the Martha Stewart Inn. And there was no guarantee that the *Gazette* would be in any hurry to bail out any of its reporters, let alone Albie.

"Come on, Snow, let's blow this dump," I said, half-dragging her toward the fields. It was a long walk to my car. "I'm putting you in my own personal witness-protection program until I can straighten this mess out."

Snow, for once, had nothing say. But I guess her

chattering teeth and noisome aroma, which filled my car nicely, said everything she had to communicate at that point.

"I'll call you!" Albie yelled. "Trust me!"

"What could possibly go wrong?" I said sourly. Why did I ask?

12

THAT'S ALL RIGHT, MAMA

OVER THE YEARS I'VE DEVELOPED MY OWN personal witness-protection program. Time or two I've had to place myself in it. So when the question of where to hide a frightened witness arises, I have an answer.

Snow was whining, "He tried to kill me. He tried to kill me!"

"Shut up, I'm trying to think," I snapped unkindly.

I was considering enlisting either my mom or Toby for what I knew was going to be a long twenty-four hours, when my evil demon of impulse whispered in my shell-pink ear and threw me a brilliant idea.

Jolene lived in Meadow Muffin Acres, one of those cutesy little town house condo deals like Friendly's

that I hate and despise as blots on the cultural landscape. It had a name like Gingerbread Court or Doily
Way or Misty Lane and looked like the Disney version of an English village, so you can just imagine.
Pounding on Jolene's Wedgwood-blue door at an un-
godly hour of the night really appealed to every mean
bone in my body, and I have quite a few.

I hoped the neighbors were all watching as I stood
on the doorstep with a puke-splattered crack skank in
tow, eyeing the stuffed teddy bear, angel, and heart-
spattered wreath with fear and loathing. Whoever invented the glue gun has a lot to answer for.

"Are you sure I'll be safe here?" Snow whined,
scratching her tattoos. She peered at the shrubbery, as
if homicidal Elvii were lurking in the pyracantha, just
waiting for her. "Oh, God, I need a cigarette so bad."

"Shut up and let me do the talking," I commanded
as the door inched open a notch.

I was interested to note that Jolene slept in a cute
little I ❤ Teddy Bears nightshirt and pink rollers the
size of soda cans. Without makeup she had a blank,
naked look. And the expression in her denuded coun-
tenance was not that of a happy camper.

"What do you want—oh, my God! What are *you*
doing here with *that*?" she hissed, giving Snow the
same look she would have given animal feces. It was
only then that I recalled their deadly rivalry for homecoming queen, way back there at Santimoke High.

"Let us in or I'll start telling you and all the neighbors,'' I replied cheerfully, shoving Snow through the door in front of me.

I felt as if I had walked into my own personal private hell.

Jolene was a devoted disciple of the country craft movement. Everything not draped in pink or blue gingham was covered with delicately colored sprigged calico. Grapevine wreaths the size of truck tires decorated the wall space not occupied by wooden cutouts of geese, sunbonnet babies, Amish dolls, and enough Holstein cattle motifs to open a small dairy. Her swagged, draped, and tiered curtains would, I was sure, be called ''window treatments,'' as if they were receiving therapy.

We walked into a living room that was a white-carpeted melange of nursery-tone pastels. Needlepoint pillows beckoned: *Welcome* ❤ *Home, I* ❤ *Angels, I* ❤ *Country,* and other syrupy mottoes. But it was shelf after load-bearing shelf, exhibiting a terrifying selection of Precious Moments figurines, that held my gaze in a merciless snare. I'd never seen so many terminally winsome, hydrocephalic, big-eyed porcelain dead-baby angels in one place before. The effect was stunning, like being hit with a (Holstein?) cattle prod. She must have had every dead-baby angel ever made. I guess she spent her lonely evenings without Rig dusting them.

''Oh, I like what you've done with the place,'' I cooed. ''Those quilts just *scream* 'Made in China by the Forced Labor of Political Prisoners.' It's just *so* quaint, and I mean that ever so sincerely!''

''She stinks!'' Jolene wrinkled her nose, pointing a long false-nailed finger at Snow. ''Don't let her walk on my new white wall-to-wall carpeting!''

Well, that certainly explained Rig's new spate of rug burns, but I kept my mind focused on the matter at hand. ''I'm calling in my favors, Jolene, in case you don't remember a certain recent scene I happened to witness at the Lock and Load,'' I told her, all business. ''Remember Snow White? She needs a place to stay for a while, and she doesn't need anyone knowing where she is.''

Her reaction was just about what you would have expected from a woman who lines the toilet seats at work with paper towels before she sits down. ''Are you crazy? She can't stay here! She's a slut! She'll stink up my house!'' Jolene lowered her voice. ''She'll steal my precious Precious Moments babies! Those are valuable collectibles!''

''Well, either she stays here, or I call Mrs. Rig and tell her a long, sad story about what I saw at the Lock and Load the other day.'' I peered around. ''Can I use your phone? Is that it under the crocheted doll?''

Jolene gave me a Precious Moments look that should have turned me into a dead-baby angel on the spot. ''Is this person one of your stupid stories?'' she demanded.

''Probably,'' I answered blithely. ''Look, all you

need to do is keep her under wraps for a while. Give her a shower and some food and clean up after her. You and Rig can do that much, can't you?''

Jolene thrust out her lower lip in a pout. It probably did wonders for Rig. It didn't work on me.

"Okay." I sighed. "You do this and we're even. My lips are sealed forever."

"I don't know what Rig will say," she offered uncertainly.

"Just tell him to bring over lots of towels, rubber gloves, and bleach when he comes. Watch out for the body fluids; you never know!" I was already on my way out. "And don't answer the door either. Someone's trying to kill her."

Jolene squawked, but I was out of the house before she could grab me. I really don't want to believe that she would have brained me with that reproduction cast-iron doorstop she had grabbed up.

As I ran for the car, I heard the sound of Snow retching and what sounded a lot like the crash of a cabinetload of Precious Moments hitting the white wall-to-wall carpeting.

Jolene had a scream that could cut steel, I noted as I pulled out of the parking lot.

THE ESSENCE OF BROOKS BROTHERS' SHIRT TRUMPETED his presence like a public-service announcement. I wasn't especially surprised when Sam appeared in the front seat of my car. "Good work," he chuckled. "Now Snow is safe and we're on the case, Holl!"

I glanced at him. Boy, it felt good to have Sam back. "So far, so good," I said. "Now what?"

He gave me the thumbs-up sign. "Takin' care of bidness," he said agreeably. "The '68 Comeback Concert, the second great incarnation. Tan, rested, dieted, and ready to rock and roll."

"So where do we rock and roll to next?" I asked reasonably.

Sam leaned back and closed his eyes, a satisfied grin playing on his handsome features. "How's about the drive-through window at Mickey D's?" he asked. "Making up always gives me an appetite. You wouldn't believe how cold it is out there in that grave-yard, or how dull either. Nobody to talk to, nothing to do but lie around all day and sulk."

"I missed you too," I said.

THE SLACK-JAWED KID AT THE DRIVE-UP WINDOW looked hard at me as I took the two number-three combos from him. I watched his eyes slide to the backseat, do a double take and a blink, then slide back to me again, then back to the backseat. He went pale beneath his acne.

"Thank you," I said briskly and hit the gas.

Sometimes people who can see ghosts don't be-lieve what they're seeing, because they don't believe in ghosts. Then they think there's something wrong with you, and that's when the trouble starts.

I didn't slow down until we were down at the waterfront, where the old canneries were. It was peaceful and deserted; no one ever came down here after dark. In the boom days this had been quite a lively area, with commercial boat traffic up and down the Santimoke River all the time. Now the canneries were shut down and the packing houses nearly obsolete as the seafood industry declined and agriculture was replaced with condos like Jolene's. The huge fields that had once produced tomatoes and corn were now covered with Meadow Muffin Acres clones. The days when produce and seafood had been shipped from here up to Baltimore were long gone, leaving behind these sad, huge buildings, more ghostly than the spirit who sat beside me, inhaling serial Big Macs in the cold moonlight.

"Thank you, thank you very much. All you've got in the backseat is half a cheese sandwich two days older than God and some mints. Hollis, do you ever think about cleaning out the back of your car?"

"Hardly ever," I told him cheerfully. "Rule of thumb: A good reporter never has a clean car. You see a reporter with a clean car, you have a bad writer, a lazy journalist, and someone who plays fast and loose with the facts."

Sam chuckled. "Sounds like some o' those people used to write about Elvis for the tabs, huh?"

"Did he *really* impregnate a UFO alien to have a Bigfoot baby?"

Sam just grinned that crooked grin. "Ask him. Stick with me, baby, and I'll give you the story of your career!"

"Trouble is, no one will believe me." I sighed. He was right; I did have a gold mine in this story, if anyone would ever believe it. "I ATE OYSTER STEW WITH ELVIS'S GHOST—now, that's a headline you could make up in woods."

"Well, you could sell it to the *Weekly World News.*" Sam tried to lick the salt off his fingers. "Living or dead, a man does love his cheeseburgers," he said happily. I could only nod, awed. I watched the man inhale a Quarter Pounder without taking a breath and demolish two bags of fries. My dead ex was an expensive date.

"Better than peanut butter and bananas." He sighed contentedly.

"Speaking of peanut-butter-and-banana sandwiches, there's still the matter of who tried to kill Snow, and who killed Bang Bang," I reminded him gently.

Sam inhaled some fries thoughtfully, if a ghost may be said to inhale thoughtfully. Maybe you had to be there.

"Look around you," he said. "What do you see?"

"Old canning houses, old packing sheds, asphalt, deserted buildings."

"What else?"

I looked around. I saw the end of the street that started on the other side of town and ran into the river. I saw the old, skeletal pilings of the wharves where the steamboats had put in, sticking up out of the cold night river like giants' fingers. I saw the single, sad streetlight that some kid had knocked out with a BB gun a long time ago. I saw the light through the broken windows and gaping frames of the old sheds and canneries; the mounds of rusting, postindustrial machinery; cog wheels and steamer baskets and all the detritus of a forgotten time.

"I see the past," I said finally. It was like high school: I didn't know if I was giving the answer that was wanted, but I was giving the answer I knew, and often the two weren't the same. "I don't see the future."

Sam raised his hands in front of himself, touching his thumbs together to frame the scene like a filmmaker. "Picture lots of bright lights and neon down here, like the carnival has come to town and stayed. Picture plastic and Naugahyde and music goin' on all the time and the jingle of slot machines and the slap of cards on the table. Picture maybe a thousand or so cars, all looking for a place to park, and all kinds of people gamblin' and drinkin' and eatin', havin' a great old time, just feedin' them slots or playin' blackjack or five-card draw, and innit that somethin'? Goin' all day and all night?"

"There's nothing I enjoy more than a pack of badly dressed people who can't afford it pumping all their money into a speculation that is geared to pay ninety-five percent to the house and five percent to the mark. I enjoy prostitution, crime, gambling addiction, and a whole other set of social and environmental problems about as much as I would enjoy a hysterectomy with a rusty spoon." I gave him a sideways glance and noted idly that his eyes, always so blue, seemed especially thoughtful tonight. Even so, they glittered in the moonlight. "You like that?" I asked dubiously.

Sam shrugged. "Doesn't matter what I do or don't like. You stop worryin' about that stuff when you die. For a ghost, everything just *is*."

"That's not what Elvis says."

"Elvis?" Sam shook his head. "The King doesn't know the half of it. He's just as famous in the other world as he is in this one." He inhaled some more fries. "Being a good ghost takes time. Patience. Learning. But you're not answering my question."

"I'm not at all certain what you want me to look for."

"The truth, Holl, the truth. You mortals can be a little ironheaded sometimes." It was a statement of fact, not a put-down. "Think, Holl, think." Sam sighed. "Who would stand to profit if this were all bought up and turned into a gambling casino?"

"Rolley Shallcross, who bought up the old canneries," I replied. "I can't figure out how a guy who's got to have a trustee could find the money or the smarts to buy real estate. But the county council shot down any idea of gambling in Santimoke County."

"For now," Sam hinted.

"Well, there will be another election next year."

"And four years after that, and four years after that."

I pondered this, turning over the possibilities. "Sooner or later it is possible that someone who favored a casino in Watertown would come into office. It could happen. Talk about more jobs, more money pumped into the economy. But the jobs are all minimum wage, and the money goes into the hands of a few out-of-state people who don't spend it around here. Meanwhile, the entire character of a nice old town and a basically rural community is changed into something looking like the boardwalk in Ocean City. Not to mention the stress on an already fragile ecosystem from increased traffic, population, and crime. Yuck," I pontificated.

"Something like that."

"But where does Bang Bang fit into all of this?" I finally asked. "Why kill him?"

Sam shrugged. "I'm just a ghost, Holl, not a psychic." He looked at his reflection—or lack of it— in the mirror and carefully inspected the arrangement of his hair. Then he gave me a sly, sideways glance.

"But even I know that where there's a stink, there's usually a dead skunk."

"Okay," I agreed.

"Consider this, then: It's an ill wind that blows no good."

"Huh?"

"Ill Wind. Isn't that the name of Rolley Shallcross's place over on Mandrake Neck?" Sam asked me patiently. "Isn't that what you told me?"

"Yeah," I answered thoughtfully. "Do you think that's worth a visit tomorrow?"

Sam grinned. "No time like the present," he said.

"But it's the middle of the night!" I protested. "Oh, no, you don't!"

"It doesn't matter, Holl," Sam promised me. "Let's go check 'er on out! Have I ever steered you wrong?"

"Countless times." I bit my lip. "But you know, we can't just waltz into a place in the middle of the night and start asking questions."

"No, but we can snoop," Sam said slyly.

ILL WIND.

The sign swung back and forth on its chains at the end of the lane though the woods.

When you drive down those long, long lanes from the road to the water, you never know what you'll find at the end. Could be a three-hundred-year-old redbrick Palladian, could be some Philip Johnson concrete number that looks like a YMCA. They all have names; trust the nouveau riche to name their acre on the water something cute. At this new, pricey end of the county, carved from old farms and estates, you could expect almost anything.

"I'm not real sure about this," I said as I turned the Honda up the asphalt drive that wound through the recently clear-cut woods. The shattered remains of tree trunks and piled-up brush that defined an area of recently harvested timber looked like a war zone. With the price of paper sky-high, lots of people had decided that spending the next twenty or thirty years waiting for new trees to grow was worth a thousand bucks an acre. "Habitat for seven million species of insects, birds, amphibians, and animals destroyed," I grumbled. "Not to mention plants and trees."

"Are you one a them tree-huggers?" Sam teased.

"Don't get me started," I told him firmly.

At least we had a clear view of a house at the end of the lane or, at the least, its silhouette looming in the moonlight. Not that it really loomed. It was a one-story rancher, probably a prefab job. It wasn't all that big, or that grand, I noted as we approached. It could have been right at home in any suburban housing development. It's very ordinariness seemed out of place and, somehow, creepy.

"I don't see any lights on," I whispered. For some

reason I felt as if raising my voice would be a bad thing.

"Don't see any cars either," Sam said. There was a hint of uneasiness in his voice too. Not a good sign.

I rolled the car window down when we pulled up to the house. The only sound was the lap of water on the shoreline and the slow, steady thumping of something swinging back and forth in the wind from the creek. In the moonlight everything was dark and blue, except the sparkle of light on the water beyond the house. In the distance I saw the silvery outline of a large cabin cruiser moored offshore.

"Okay," I said. "We found out where Shallcross lives. Now let's go before he comes outta the house with a shotgun and starts firing at us."

"I think we oughta take a look around," Sam said, but he didn't sound as certain about it as he had back at the waterfront in town. "I mean, as long as we're here 'n' all."

"Yeah, but I feel as if when we get outta the car, that's when he'll drive up. Or come flying out of the house with a shotgun."

Sam thought about this for a moment. "Naaa," he said. "Come on, Holl. It'll be fun!"

"Easy for you to say. You're a dead guy. Nothin's gonna happen to you!" I was about to put the car into gear and get the hell outta there when Sam held up a hand.

"Listen!" he said urgently.

I listened.

"Don't you hear that?" Sam asked.

I listened.

"That's the Mandrake Shoal bell," Sam said. He lifted himself off the seat and through the passenger door of the car. "It tolls only in fog or when the creek is icing up. Come on, Holl, the game is afoot!"

"Oh, man!" I sighed. But I got out of the car and followed him to the house.

Sam disappeared through the front door. Just slid right through the solid wood.

In a second I saw his face appear in one of the glass panes above my head. "Door's unlocked," he told me.

I took a deep breath and went into someone else's house.

It was pitch black inside, but as my eyes adjusted to the darkness, I discerned pools of moonlight on the floor, streaming in through the windows. The smell of someone else's life: Fried food, stale wood smoke, wet wool, and something more repulsive assailed my nose.

"Now what?" I asked Sam, who was standing a few feet away from me, the moonlight filtering gently through his body, glimmering on his blue shirt and chino pants.

"I dunno," he said uncertainly. "I thought I heard someone moaning, but now I'm not so sure."

I reached out and touched the wall beside the door.

I felt a stiff lampshade and the table beneath it and fumbled for the light switch.

Illumination flooded a dark hallway, paneled with cheap dark siding. I was dimly aware of rooms on either side and dim shapes in the darkness.

"Now what?" I asked Sam.

"I guess we look around a little—"

I tried another wall switch.

Bad move.

It felt like an explosion. Suddenly, everything seemed to be bathed in swirling lights—red, pink, blue, yellow, green neon like eye slaps. And the sound of Elvis singing "Blue Suede Shoes" blared out from every wall, so loud that I had to clap my hands over my ears.

Sam, however, seemed to be enjoying it. He snapped his fingers and did some pelvic thrusts as if we were in a disco. "Ooooh, yeaaaah, baby, that's music!" he yelled. "Go, cat, go!" He danced around the floor.

It took me a second to figure out that the music was coming from an ancient Wurlitzer jukebox in the room to the right. Evidently, I'd found the toggle that turned on the juke.

I stumbled toward it, looking for a way to turn it off. I was utterly certain that the damned thing was some kind of burglar alarm from hell.

In the dim light it cast, I became aware that the room was some kind of shrine. Muted lights illumi-

nated a sort of altar featuring a large painting on velvet as the object of adoration. Artificial flowers were
piled around the bottom of it, and tiny votive candles
flickered in small niches around the frame. I squinted
at the subject of the painting. At first I had thought it
was a *santo* or the Virgin Mary, but I was wrong. It
was a painting of Elvis on velvet.

"It's the apotheosis of Elvis," I breathed. "Boy, I
wish he could see this!"

"Isn't that nice?" my companion remarked.

The whole room was a shrine to the King. Elvis
stuff was everywhere, stacked head high, piled on the
furniture, covering the floor, save for a narrow path-
way to the jukebox. It was, I noted, all Elvisiana, all
the time; records and movie posters and paintings on
velvet and cookie jars and commemorative plates and
neon wall clocks and couch throws and full-size cutouts of the King. If Mojo Nixon is right and Elvis is
everybody and Elvis is everywhere, then we must
have fallen into the Elvis black hole in the universe.

I eased gingerly farther into the room, as if com-
pelled by the force of gravity. Or as if I'd fallen into
Alice's rabbit hole. The face of the King stared down
at me from every wall. On T-shirts, in posters, from
vinyl-record covers, magazine clippings, baseball
caps; anything that could have Elvis's face on it did.

"Jesus," Sam said, not entirely irreverently.

"No, Elvis," I replied. "But for somebody,

they're interchangeable deities. Elvis, the Protestant Saint, the God of Excess—''

"Don't get philosophical on me now," Sam commanded.

Turning, I stumbled and fell over something large, furry, and cold on the floor. As I tripped I assumed it was some kind of dog.

It was only when I found myself flat on my stomach, staring at a dead and glassy eye, that I realized that this wasn't a dog.

It was a very dead Rolley Shallcross.

A bright red scarf was wrapped around his neck.

But I was pretty certain it was the neat black bullet hole in the middle of his forehead that had done him in.

13

SUSPICIOUS MINDS

"GAACK!" I EXCLAIMED, ROLLING AWAY from the corpse. "He's dead!" My talent for stating the obvious appalls even me, but the man was definitely defunct and probably had been for a while. If Jolene thought Snow White had bad hygiene, she should have smelled this guy. He was rank, having voided his bowels and bladder. And the fact that he'd been shot in the head didn't make looking at him in the greenish neon light of a jukebox any more pleasant.

" 'Oh, that this too mortal flesh would melt away,' " Sam quoted.

"Very funny," I snarled as I got to my feet and backed as far away from the dead man as I could before I slammed into a life-size cutout of the

King from his God of Excess Vegas years. "Now what?"

"Well," Sam said thoughtfully, "it looks to me as if we have a choice. We either get the hell out of here and pretend we never came, or we call the po-lice, specifically your pal Friendly, and wait for them to take over."

"Let's get out of here first," I suggested. I really wished I hadn't fallen over the corpse. "I need some fresh air."

Outside, I gulped down fresh air. I knew the cold would hurt my lungs, but I didn't care. "You and your big ideas," I huffed and puffed at Sam. I wondered if I was going to be sick.

"Well, how was I to know he was dead?" Sam asked in such a reasonable tone of voice that I wished I could shoot *him*.

"There's only one thing we can do," I decided. "I have to call Friendly. Not 911, just Friendly. Sure, he'll be furious with me, but there's a murdered man in there, and if it's Rolley Shallcross, which it looks like it is—was—whatever!" My teeth were chattering. "Then that would let Albie off the hook, because he doesn't have any reason to kill Shallcross."

"That you know of," Sam muttered with an angelic look. "This is all starting to follow a pattern of Elvisness. First there's Bang Bang Devine, strangled with the sort of scarf Elvis used to mop his fevered brow, then handed out to fans. Then tonight someone tried to snuff Snow White—I wonder where she was when I was a horny teen—with a peanut-butter-and-banana sandwich, fave fare of the King. And now we find what looks like Rolley Shallcross, shot with a gun just the way the King used to blast out the talking heads who annoyed him on TV. Maybe Elvis Man talked too much? Shallcross—if, indeed, that is him in there—seems to have been done to death in the very temple of Elvis, Elvis the gun nut, a human sacrifice to the God of Excess, hmmm?''

''Dying for Elvis,'' I murmured. ''All around the big Elvis weekend. Sam, we don't have a choice; I have to call Friendly.''

I dug around in my pocketbook for my phone. Unfortunately, when I tried to get a dial tone, it burped and beeped and crackled static in my ear.

''It's breaking up, dammit,'' I said. ''Maybe if I go around to the side of the house, I can get a better signal.''

''You can try,'' Sam said. ''I'm getting out of here, personally. The last thing I need is a pack of cops. I'll catch you later.''

So saying, he turned to mist and fog.

''Terrific,'' I snapped. ''When I really need you, you always seem to find somewhere else to be!'' Still crankily muttering to myself, I moved cautiously through the dark around the side of the house. I tried several locations, but none of them rewarded me with much more than static. Perhaps the same electric system that controlled all the bells and whistles in the Elvis room was interfering with my cell-phone reception. What do I look like, Radio Shack? I don't know how these things work, and the one person who could possibly tell me had conveniently cut out for parts unknown.

Finally, I moved all the way down to the water. There I was rewarded with a clear dial tone. I took a deep breath of the arctic air blowing across the water, looking without really seeing the water. The cabin cruiser still rode at her moorings, painter stretched taut against the wind. There was something about that boat that I should look at, I thought dimly. Just then my phone belched out a clear dial tone.

I was just punching in Friendly's cell-phone number when I heard a roar coming at me from nowhere.

Then my worst nightmare came true.

I turned just in time to see a car barreling across the lawn.

I was frozen in the headlights like a deer, watching the behemoth roll right at me.

I squeaked, jumping out of the way inches from the enormous chrome grille, which looked like an open maw. I could feel the smooth metal of the fender brush against my hip as it lumbered past my legs, missing me by just inches. "Hey!" I yelled. "Watch it!"

It wasn't just any car. It was a giant pink Cadillac of fifties' vintage, tailfins bearing down on me like a land shark as it was thrown into reverse, red taillights blinking evil eyes as it rolled back toward me, *fast.*

I was being run down by an Elvismobile.

''Sam! Help!'' I yelled, spinning out of the way as the Caddy rolled backward and passed me. I heard its transmission grinding as it shifted into forward gear again and steered toward me, gathering speed.

I ran.

I was too far from the house to seek shelter in the shrubbery. Besides, that thing would take out the azaleas and half a wall—and me along with them—without even making a dent in that gleaming silver and pink fender. The Caddy's big V8 engine roared like a bull as it lumbered toward me at warp speed. I couldn't see the driver's face. I couldn't see anything but the headlights.

Satchel Paige was right, I remember thinking. I shouldn't have looked behind me, because something *was* catching up with me. And because I was watching it, instead of where I was going, I tripped and fell, sprawling over the frozen grass.

Several tons of pink steel were flying right at me as I struggled to roll out of the way. It looked as if I were going to meet an untimely end as a bug on the windshield of life. That car looked as big as an elephant bearing down on my helpless form.

Then a miracle happened. The Cadillac lurched to a stop with a loud clunk. The high-beams suddenly focused toward the sky, the enormous tail fins dropped several feet, and the wheels began to spin helplessly, spewing out mud and grass.

The death car had rolled right over the septic tank. All that gross tonnage was too much weight for the soft earth over the cesspool. Several tons of metal lurching repeatedly over the drain field had weakened the soft earth and created a hole big enough to sink the car's rear end.

I figured that all out just before I scrambled to my feet and sprinted off into the ruins of the woods. It was the longest thirty-foot run I'd ever made in my life, hitting the edge of the woods as if it was my last hope of salvation—which, at that point, maybe it was. Not even a Cadillac could penetrate a forest of stumps, dead branches, and downed trees.

Behind me, the monster's transmission whined as it ground itself deeper and deeper into the soft earth. Rocking back and forth in a vain attempt to work free just sunk it in even deeper. I imagined it dropping right into the septic tank, and paused, but no such luck.

From behind me I heard a car door open and slam shut, and I took off running again into the ravaged dark landscape.

I fell over stumps and crawled over tree branches, panting and half-crying as I tried to find a place in that war zone of harvested woods to hide. Once I slid into an open hole filled with ice, scrambling to grab at the upended roots of a dead tree to pull myself free.

There was just enough moonlight for me to be seen, but not enough to see.

I stood upright, panting. I'd lost my bearings.

It was quiet. Too quiet.

Then I felt someone's hands on my shoulders, pulling me backward. Someone strong—their fingers hurt when they dug into me right through my coat, and they were propelling me backward a lot faster than I wanted to go. I saw the tail end of a red scarf in the moonlight and knew what was coming.

I hate surprises.

Isn't it interesting, the way we do what we've been trained to in an emergency without even thinking about it?

I caught my balance, yelled "Aaaaiiiiiiiieeeeee!" and grabbed his pinky fingers, bending them back as hard as I could. When he yelled and let go of me, I turned and grabbed his groin and squeezed. He howled and went down. "Aaaaiiiiiiiieeeeee!" I kept yelling too.

All I saw was Elvis. The wig, the shades, the jumpsuit, up and clutching his testicles and hopping around.

So I did the most natural thing in the world and whacked Elvis upside his head with my pocketbook, just as I'd been taught at Miss Patti's Christian School of Tap and Ballet's Self-Defense for Ladies class. And I blessed my mother, who'd forced me to go with her. Patti you don't want to mess with, since she'll pray for you while she's poking out your eyes with her car keys.

Talk about muscular Christianity.

My entire life is carried around in my pocketbook; the five pounds of loose change in the bottom alone gives it a weight and heft. Add my wallet, with another pound of loose change, a checkbook stuffed with receipts and coupons, two or three reporter notebooks, four thousand assorted business cards, half a bottle of Evian water, tins of Altoids, two hundred pens—some of which even work—a change of underwear, two Tampax, a penknife, a comb, school photos of my niece and nephew and my several godchildren (always a godmother, never a god is my story), a couple of cheap paperbacks, and most of the mail from the past month. Well, anyway, you get the idea.

I slugged Elvis with fifteen pounds of ratty old Coach bag, and he fell inward like an imploded building.

Just as I thought I'd committed rock and roll regicide, Elvis grunted and picked himself up. All I saw was *something* with a wad of hot buttered yak wool on its head loping off into the long, moonlit shadows where the woods used to be, with his hands between his legs.

But I wasn't about to stick around to enjoy my victory. I grabbed my cell phone and clutched my bag and got the hell into my car and locked all the doors and headed out of there with the pedal to the metal and I didn't stop until I got to the general store five miles down to the crossroad.

It was closed up tighter than Jesse Helms's mind, but the floodlights were on and the parking lot was well-lit.

I waited until I could catch my breath and utter a simple declarative sentence, and then I called Friendly.

I WAS STILL SITTING IN THE CAR WITH THE WINDOWS rolled up and locked, clutching my Buck knife and my cell phone and shaking like a leaf, when he showed up with a posse seven minutes later. Just hearing those sirens wailing in the distant night comforted me.

The what-ifs were starting to set in. What if he'd hit me with that five-ton car? What if I hadn't been able to whack the guy? What if he'd been armed? What if, what if, what if, what if . . .

"Oh, my God," I moaned.

A good imagination is a curse.

Friendly jumped out of his cherry-red Ranchero faster than I would have thought he could move. By the expression on his face, I knew that he had a good imagination too.

In one of those moments of epiphany that strikes in times of stress, it suddenly occurred to me that he

really did care about me. I opened the door and collapsed into his arms.

"Are you okay?" he demanded, looking me all
over like an anxious mother cat.

"Just really sh-sh-shaken up," I managed to say,
taking a lot of deep breaths. "S-s-scared to death, but
okay."

Friendly shook his head, and I knew as fear turned
to relief that he was going to go ballistic next, which
he did. His green eyes narrowed, the lines in his face
hardened, and he starting to turn an interesting shade
of red. Nothing you can say will take the anger away
from my guy.

"What the hell were you doing out there?" he demanded. "I told you to stay the hell away from this
case!"

I really didn't have an answer for that one, and I
was too rattled to come up with a good lie. So I did
the next best thing and broke down in tears, which
would have been a really smooth move, except that I
wasn't kidding. I'd just had the bejesus scared out of
me. And what's more, I'd found out that I wasn't as
tough as I thought I was, which was very depressing.

It was even more depressing to have Harve and a
bunch of county deputies and M.S.P. troopers watch
me cry and shake like a June bride at a tent revival.
Life *is* one humiliation after another, especially for
me, in case you haven't noticed.

But Friendly didn't want to hear about my self-revelations. He was too busy barking orders to the boys in the cruiser and Harve, who took off for Ill Wind with sirens blaring and gumballs flashing.

"Must have been a dull night in Santimoke County," I remarked, watching them go. "Looks like everybody and their mom turned out for this one. Dippy Donut's receipts must have dropped twenty-five points."

"Don't make jokes, Hollis," he said tightly, pushing his hands deep into his pockets and frowning at me. "We've probably lost whoever it was by now, but you could have been hurt or even killed. Then what?"

"I dunno," I replied. I wished I could stop shaking. "Should I register my pocketbook as a deadly weapon?"

Friendly hefted it off my shoulder, weighing it with one finger hooked in the strap. "Good Lord, what do you carry in there?"

"I'm glad I didn't go for my gun," I replied. "I could have shot myself while I was trying to dig it out."

"This isn't funny," Friendly growled. He proceeded to give me a dressing-down that was both inventive and colorful and full of threats about charging me with obstruction and a lot of other stuff. It *would* have been funny if I hadn't felt so scared and guilty. I really tried to turn off the waterworks, but I kept sniffling, which Friendly, like most men, has a really hard time dealing with. After a while I was crying as much from frustration as fear, and then I got the hiccups, which made it even worse.

Finally, Friendly, having exhausted his temper, handed me a box of Kleenex, and I wiped my running nose and teary eyes.

"You know," he said, "some women really look cute when they cry. You don't."

"Thanks," I sniffled. "I will admit that it's nice to have a big strong chest to lean against, however."

"Arr," Friendly growled, but he did keep hugging me. "You've lived through worse. Come on, let's go take a look at this corpse of yours."

Men are *so* good at dealing with your feelings.

"ELVIS IN A CADILLAC?" HARVE REPEATED SLOWLY, looking at me with his head to one side, his gold tooth glittering. "You were attacked by Elvis in that Cadillac out there? It's déjà vu all over again. Wasn't there that Cadillac that sank in the river. You were there for that too. What is it with you and Caddies?"

We both stole a look out the window at the pink Eldorado mired in what had been the Ill Wind cesspool. Illuminated by several rescue-squad vans and a tow truck, it looked more pathetic than lethal, a big old fifties' Elvismobile coated in other people's personal history. The smell was intense. Happily, we were upwind of the house, which had its own noisome problems.

"Then Elvis jumped out an' tried to mug you?" Harve sounded skeptical, and who could blame him?

"Gimme a break, Harve." I sighed. "He just looked like Elvis. You know, the wig, the shades, the jumpsuit. It was a disguise, I guess—I dunno. He tried to run me down, then got out of the car and grabbed me in the dark. Snuck up on me."

Harve shrugged. "Whatever. I was just wondering, because it sounds, like—" He waved his hands around in the air, nonplussed.

"Yeah, I know," I said. "That's how it looked too. All Elvii look the same in the dark. In the daylight too. It's the perfect disguise when there are about fifty of 'em runnin' around town."

"The boys'll make a run on the tags." Harve sighed. "Jesus, Hollis." He shook his head.

I cast a look at the corpse on the floor, mercifully just an anthropomorphic lump beneath a woven coverlet someone had thrown over him.

With anticipation we all watched as someone unloaded the frail and diminutive Santimoke County medical examiner from the back of a county cruiser. The jingle of the miniature bottles stashed in his pockets announced his advent to all, and all sound and motion ceased. Doc Westmore, whose legendary vodka consumption had long ago proscribed practice on live patients, was still being hauled out for unattended deaths where the harm had already been done.

With careful drunken dignity the little old man tiptoed on his tiny wing tips across the floor and peered down at the cloth draped over the corpse.

A tech lifted the coverlet, and Doc peered myopically into the blackened, bloated face of the deceased.

Taking a pen from his pocket, he hooked the cloth and held it up to the light, inspecting the famous face imprinted on the spread rather than the corpse it covered.

"Gennelman," he announced, "what we've got here is the Shroud of Elvis."

He dropped the spread over the body again. "Rolley Shallcross. Dead as a rockfish," he pronounced. "Gunshot to the head. Maybe within the past twenty-four hours, probably less. Take him away, boys." He fumbled in a pocket, withdrew an airline-size bottle of Stoly, and downed it in one swallow before ambling away to stare at the collection of you-know-who stuff that filled the house.

Harve shook his head, choking back a laugh as he made up the paperwork for Doc to sign.

A collective sigh filled the room as people started about their business again.

"You heard Doc." Harve gestured to the techs. "He's dead as a rockfish. Do your stuff. Dead white male, approximate age mid-thirties to high forties, name—pending formal ID—Rolley Shallcross. R-o-l-l—"

"I thought it would be that other fella," Doc said peevishly, eyeing Friendly over his wire-rimmed

glasses. He held an Elvis cookie jar at the length of
his arms, shaking his head.

"What other fella?"

Doc drew himself up to his full five feet. "That
fella who fell off the boat."

Everyone looked at him blankly as he carefully
placed the cookie jar back on a shelf loaded with
other improbable objects adorned with likenesses of
the King.

Doc picked at one of the embroidered mallards on
his jacket. "You recall that fella, that lawyer fella that
fell off the boat? Zip? Flip? Fop?"

"Zap Gadsen?" Friendly asked, puzzled.

"That's the one." Doc opened another miniature
and took a swallow, eyeing a wall covered with
Elvis's record jackets. "Never could stand that Presley fella," he added conversationally. "Moved his
hips too much."

"Now, Doc, what d'you know about Zap Gadsen?" Harve asked reasonably. "This here is Elvis
Man."

"I know a Shallcross when I see one! I delivered
that boy! He was a change-of-life baby, poor thing.
But I know that Gadsen fella too. He lives here. I've
been prescribing his pills for him for the past two
years, haven't I?" Doc demanded querulously.
"Ought to know my own damned patients. Only have
two or three left, and one of them was that Gadsen
fella." He glanced at the late Rolley Shallcross. "I

thought it would be that lawyer; he *must* have been sick for all the pills he wanted. Poor Rolley wasn't all there, but he was healthy as a horse.''

"Doc," Harve explained gently, "Zap Gadsen drowned two years ago. You couldn't prescribe for him. He's been takin' his meds from the big drugstore in the sky for quite a while now.''

"To hell he is! He's been taking medicine for his nerves for two years, regular as clockwork. I just saw him last week!'' Doc turned his basilisk stare on poor Harve.

"But, Doc, Zap Gadsen drowned two years ago. They never found the body!''

"I guess that's because he's been here, stayin' inside this house for two years. You know, I made house calls on him.''

I don't know which idea was worse, Doc driving or Doc prescribing for a man we all assumed was crab food by now.

"No, we didn't know. Doc, the man was supposed to be missing. I think he'd been declared dead. Why didn't you tell anyone?'' someone asked.

Doc Westmore gave them all a good glaring at. "Because," he said simply, "no one ever asked me!''

14

I'M LEFT, YOU'RE RIGHT, SHE'S GONE

"NOBODY ASKED HIM," FRIENDLY SAID FOR perhaps the twentieth time. "Here he is, treating a man who disappeared off the face of the earth—it was in all the papers and on TV—and Doc didn't think anyone needed to know about it." He shook his head. "It's not a region, it's a goddamned *cult,* this goddamned Eastern Shore."

Harve dipped his doughnut into his coffee, then bit into it thoughtfully. Under the harsh lights of Dippy Donut, he looked even younger than he really was. "How do we know it's really Elvis Man? We need a positive ID," he offered with his mouth full.

"We'll get hold of his cousin and *get* a goddamned positive ID," Friendly replied moodily. "What happened to Gadsen? He must still be alive, he must be out there somewhere, dammit. If Doc's right he's been hiding out at Shallcross's house all this time. Why the hell would Rolley let him stay there? Are you sure that you didn't get a good look at the driver? What is it with you and Cadillacs? You have a beef with GM or something?'' These were the first words he'd spoken directly to me since we'd left Ill Wind. At least he was speaking to me now, even if it was to bark.

"All I saw was the Caddy, then the Elvis drag," I replied wearily for the twentieth time. "It all happened so *fast*. I was scared to death. I still am. At least this means Albie didn't do it!" I crowed.

"He's been released from questioning, but he's not off the hook yet," Friendly growled, not looking at me. "We don't have an official time of death for Shallcross till the real M.E. up in Baltimore makes a ruling. And there weren't any plates on the car, not even historical tags. Apparently, the Eldorado was a collector's item, not a car you could actually drive somewhere. Shallcross canceled the insurance on it and turned in the tags when he bought it. It was supposed to have been a gift Elvis gave to a friend, but who knows? Why in hell anyone would want to run you down with a car that's worth more than you are, I don't know!" He gave a surly grunt and bit into his doughnut.

I had to be content with that. And I was smart enough, for once, not to pursue it. I didn't blame

Friendly for being in a crappy mood. He had been so certain that Albie'd killed Bang Bang, and now he had a fresh corpse on his hands and an Elvis on the loose, attacking women with high cholesterol and heavy metal. I shuddered again, thinking about that grotesque trying to run me down, then strangle me.

"More blueberry glaze, hon?" Friendly pushed a doughnut at me, but I wasn't really interested in anything even vaguely healthy. But at least it was a thin end of the wedge of forgiveness.

Good old Dippy Donut. Where else around here could you eat from the four major food groups at 2:00 A.M.? I had certainly enjoyed my helpings of carbs, sugar, cholesterol, and fat. There's nothing like finding a corpse and being attacked by Elvis to make me crave a glazed double-creme chocolate. With sprinkles.

"We'll go over the area again in daylight with the cadets," Friendly told Harve. "We could have missed almost anything in the dark." They'd left guards around the place, so it was doubtful my attacker would be sneaking back to pick up any spare clues he may have dropped around the yard. He certainly hadn't escaped in the Eldorado. They'd given up trying to figure out how to leverage the damned thing out of the drain field tonight; apparently it was down in there pretty deep. There was some talk of bringing in a crane tomorrow, but meanwhile, I hoped no one wanted to flush any toilets out there.

Harve was nodding thoughtfully, his expression screwed around the way it is when he's ruminating. "I've never seen anything like this, Sarge," he said around a mouthful of cranberry buttermilk delite. "It's almost like we got an Elvis serial killer on our hands. Mebbe we should call in the F.B.I.?"

"No Feebies," Friendly groaned. "If we could just find this Zap character and verify that he's still alive. God, I hate lawyers." He took a hit from his coffee cup and shredded his paper napkin. "What I can't figure out is why Shallcross hid him. Where has Gadsen been for the past two or three years? Was he really living at Shallcross's house? Why? Did he stage his own disappearance, or was someone holding him someplace or what? Have we got a serial killer here? The Elvis disguise thing is diabolical!"

Harve scratched his head and yawned. "I'll get to work tomorrow digging into his paperwork, Sarge," he promised, making notes. "Check out his will, stuff like that. Maybe we can find a clue in what was going on when he disappeared."

"Doc says the man he calls Zap Gadsen asked for a lot of downers. Quaaludes, Seconals, stuff like that. Gave his real name. Says he can't remember when he started treating him. And Doc being Doc, he wrote out those prescriptions like barbiturates were goin' out of style. The same pills we found on the night-stand at the Lock and Load. We'll have to check and see where Gadsen had the scripts filled. The druggists may be able to give us some information.''

I sighed wearily. ''This just gets more and more complicated. But at least now you have to admit that Albie's in the clear.'' Loyal to the end, that's me.

Friendly tossed me a bald, tired look. ''I don't have to admit anything,'' he said firmly. ''And you should feel lucky that you're alive and that I don't lock you up for trespass and obstruction.''

''But it wasn't Albie who attacked me—''

''You said you couldn't ID the guy.''

''Yeah, but I know it wasn't Albie—''

''How?''

''I just know. . . .'' But I was beginning to wonder if I really did know Albie at all.

''Bullshit. Won't hold up, Hollis. Sorry.'' Friendly sipped at his coffee, staring bleakly at the racks of doughnuts behind the counter.

I bit back what I wanted to say. Because I realized that *I* couldn't say it wasn't Albie either. But why would Albie kill Rolley Shallcross? Albie wasn't the type to get bent out of shape if the sheets weren't changed. If, indeed, this was Elvis Man Shallcross I'd fallen over at Ill Wind. If it was Zap Gadsen who'd attacked me.

I took another bite of my doughnut, watching the sullen, big-haired waitress pour coffee for a couple of truck drivers, and half-listened as Friendly and Harve went over the Elvis connection again and again. And again, looking for missing pieces of the puzzle.

Friendly marveled over Doc Westmore's interpretation of patient confidentiality, and Harve tried, without success, to explain Doc Westmore, who defies any explanation. "He's just an Eastern Shoreman, that's all," Harve finally concluded limply.

"Y'know," I volunteered, "Captain Len Salmon had to testify in a maritime trial up in Baltimore one time. The plaintiff's lawyer was trying to discredit him as a witness, so he said to Captain Len, 'Well, sir, on the Eastern Shore you have a lot of characters, don't you?' You know, real patronizing, as if being a character was bad thing, and Captain Len, he comes right back and says, 'Characters? Characters? We've got characters we haven't even used yet!' The jury," I added, "ruled in favor of the defendant."

Friendly shot me an unreadable look. "Can I get some more coffee down here?" he asked the waitress, who growled something at him as two Elvii, as alike as two *P*'s in a Presley, drifted past in search of midnight snacks. I guess since the Lock and Load was right next door it made sense for them to waft through here.

Friendly watched them for a moment, then observed, "*There*'s a character we haven't used yet."

We followed his gaze and watched as none other than Vera Devine sashayed into the Dippy Donut. She was trailing scarves and dripping necklaces of semiprecious stones. This night she was a vision in bohemian black. She must have picked up Albie, for he was trailing right behind her.

My godfather looked just plain worn out. I guessed they'd really put him through it out at the barracks. He was toting Vera's extra shawls and bags like a hired hand, walking two steps behind. As we watched she peeled off a big black cape and handed it to him, then stripped off her gloves, which she dumped on top of the pile in his arms without even looking at him. Instead, she scanned the room, looking as if something smelled bad. I guess we did.

When Vera and Albie saw us, they stood rooted to the spot for a moment, obviously none too pleased. We were all flashing each other looks.

"Hard at work, huh?" Friendly finally greeted Albie mildly.

Albie looked at me, then looked away, his deadwhite skin flushing scarlet up his hairline. I knew he was embarrassed to be seen this way. And I was hurting for him. But I was also unhappy to have been dragged into this mess and nearly killed.

It was Vera who recovered first. Her bracelets and earrings jingled as she crossed the tile floor to greet us. Her eyes, lined in kohl, were almost unreadable, but there was no New Age bliss in the look she gave us.

"Is this the only twenty-four-hour place open around here?" she asked peevishly, giving a sour look to the racks of brightly iced doughnuts. "I really don't care to eat refined sugar or drink anything with caffeine in it. Miss, miss! Yes, over here, please! Do you know if you have anything made with organic flour and honey?" she called imperiously.

I was waiting with great interest for the answer, but the waitress just turned away and said something that made the truckers laugh.

"No tip for you," I muttered, and Friendly gave me a sharp poke in the hip with his elbow.

"Well, Albie, don't just stand there, get us a table," Vera commanded, and Albie, probably glad to be out of the line of fire, grabbed a booth with a great view of the parking lot and Route 50. Several Elvii joined him there, all of them glaring at us like we were Robert Goulet impersonators.

There is something really surreal about being surrounded by Elvii at 2:00 A.M. in the Dippy Donut, but it all made sense at the time.

"I think they have herb teas," I offered. "Nearly everyone does these days."

Vera frowned. "I couldn't sleep, so I told Albie to take me over here to get a bite. My *chai* is really out of balance from all this negative energy. Very disturbing! Have you discovered who killed Bang Bang yet, Sergeant Friendly?"

"No, Mrs. Devine, but we're working on it," he replied, deadpan. He didn't mention the events at Ill Wind.

She cast a pitying look over the three of us with our evil sugar and caffeine and smiled the patronizing smile of the self-righteous health Nazi. "I certainly hope so. Neither Elvis nor I was especially pleased when you dragged Albie in for questioning. I had to go down there and pick him up. You know, Elvis is very upset by this whole thing. I haven't had a message from him in several days, and that's not like him at all." She licked her lower lip. "I think this whole thing has really upset his energy patterns."

"Well, Mrs. Devine, I know it's upset ours," Friendly told her, perfectly serious. "We're doing our best."

She regarded the three of us lined up at the counter like a trio of crows perched on a phone wire, and I could tell what she was thinking. That we should all be out there taking fingerprints or grilling the local criminal element instead of persecuting her and Albie. Since the local criminal element rolls up his glassine envelopes and goes home to watch ESPN at about eleven on weeknights, she was out of luck in the guilt department.

After eyeballing us for a couple of seconds, she swished off to join Albie and the Elvii in the booth, where they elaborately ignored us as they spoke to each other in low tones.

"I don't much like this," Friendly muttered. "Those two know more than they're letting on."

"So do we," I noted dryly.

"But we're supposed to," Harve pointed out reasonably.

"I knew that!" I snapped. "I just hope all those other Elvii are sound asleep at the Lock and Load and not out holding up banks or something."

"We've got people over there." Friendly watched Albie and Vera in the reflection of the doughnut case. The waitress took their order and shuffled away, shaking her head.

Friendly suddenly eased off his stool. Harve and I watched as he slid into the booth with Albie and Vera. Whatever he said, it made them laugh. Albie relaxed visibly, his long skinny body collapsing in on itself like a rubber band.

"Watch the old master," Harve commanded me in a low tone.

"Oh, I've been watching the old master for a long time," I replied. "That's my problem."

When Friendly came back he looked like the cat who had consumed a large helping of canary.

"What did you find out, Sarge?" Harve asked him.

Friendly smiled. "More than I bargained for, more than I bargained for." He gave me a real hard look.

Out of the corner of my eye, I noted that Albie was slinking off to the men's room, leaving Vera with her herb tea, a bran muffin, and a copy of *Cosmic Mother* magazine. No wonder she was so spacey, if that was her idea of an aftermidnight treat.

Friendly and Harve had their heads together, muttering in cop-ese, probably about whether or not to charge *me* next.

I saw my chance and I took it, picking up my bag and heading off in the direction of the bathrooms. The truckers were eyeing the Elvii with great interest.

I found Albie in the men's room locked in a stall, thank God. There are some things about my godfather I don't care to contemplate, whether he changed my diapers or not.

"Listen, Albie," I said without preamble. "I want some answers. Starting with what the pluperfect hell is going on between you and the lovely Vera. Bang Bang's not even cold in the ground yet!"

"Aw, Hollis, can't a man have any peace anywhere?" Albie's voice traveled over the top of the stall. The room had an eerie tile echo.

"Bang Bang didn't get much peace in the bathroom," I replied. "Listen here, I've been threatened with jail on account of you, and there's an Elvis out there who tried to kill me and Snow tonight. I think I deserve some answers. Let's start with what you're doing with the Widder Devine when the body's not even cold on the gurney."

Albie's pants were puddled around his ankles. The tips of his long, thin brogans twitched. "Well, it's not like I have a choice." He sighed. "She just sort of came in and took over. And I owe her ten big ones."

"So you've taken up gigolo-ing?"

"That's a hard word, Hollis," Albie's voice said

piously. "Vera's all right. Besides, I'm dead broke and she stands to inherit Bang Bang's business. Not to mention working off that ten grand. I'm offering the lady some spiritual comfort in her hour of grief," he added.

"She acts about as grief-stricken as Alan Greenspan raising interest rates," I observed. "Meanwhile, back at the ranch, somebody murdered Elvis Man, Rolley Shallcross. He was found strangled with an Elvis scarf at his house. I literally stumbled over him in the dark. The somebody then tried to run me over with a big pink Cadillac. And when that didn't work they tried to strangle me with an Elvis scarf. Any of this sound familiar yet?"

Albie didn't reply. So I pressed on.

"Zap Gadsen, Bang Bang's lawyer, who was supposed to have fallen off his sailboat and was never recovered? Well, a couple years later he turns up as a relatively alive person who scams scripts from old Doc Westmore. You wouldn't happen to know anything about that, would you? If you do you've gotta talk to Friendly. You've gotta do the right thing, Albie."

Dead silence on the other side of the stall.

"Where is Zap Gadsen, Albie? What's the connection between him and Bang and Bang and gambling in Santimoke County? Is Gadsen running around in an Elvis suit trying to kill people? Or is this some crazy thing between you and Vera? What's going on,

Albie? You've created another mess, and you've dragged some decent people into it. Frank Carroll, me, Friendly—you create a mess and we're the ones who get hit with a scandal.'' I took a deep breath. ''You really let me down here, Albie. I stood up for you and you let me down.''

There was a longer silence. I stared at the graffiti on the walls and stalls, products of transient teenagers on their way to the stews of Ocean City. Did Billy really love Tiffany, or was it just a teenage romance? Could someone named Phyllis really do that? It seemed physically impossible to me. How nice that Tough Guy Butt Fuck had left his tag here for all to see. I yawned. I was suddenly, infinitely weary.

''I ain't got nothin' to say,'' Albie replied at last. ''Now, get outta here so a man can do what a man's gotta do in private.''

I took a deep breath. ''I thought you had become a stand-up guy, but now I see you don't stand up for anything but yourself. Fuck you, Albie.''

I slammed out of the men's room just in time to witness something I never thought I would see in this lifetime.

Vera Devine was sitting in the booth, talking with the Elvii, just as she had been when I left. Only it wasn't Vera talking. Well, it was Vera, but it was as if someone else was pulling her strings, as if someone else had borrowed her voice. Someone familiar to us all.

"It's all in the moves," she was saying, only it wasn't her voice, it was Elvis's voice. And she was looking at the Elvii, her face kind of twisted up like Harve's when he's thinking hard, only it was giving her this expression, this expression like . . . Elvis. "You get the moves, see? If you wanna do me, you gotta watch stuff like the hips and the feet. It's all in the hips and the feet—" Suddenly, she broke off and looked right at me as I passed by. Or, rather—and follow me here, because this is really weird—E looked at me. The ghost from Toby's bar, only it was as if he were using Vera's body. I almost passed out when she/he said, "Hey, Hollis, you workin' on findin' my blue suede shoes?" And she/he winked.

"That didn't happen," I said and kept right on walking. Either Vera was for real with the channeling Elvis thing, or the crystal cruncher was a better actress than I thought she was. Either way I didn't want to know.

Friendly and Harve barely glanced up as I took my stool at the counter again. ". . . chances looked about the same as a snowball's in hell—" Harve was saying.

"Oh, my God!" I exclaimed. "Snow White! I forgot all about her!"

15
RETURN TO SENDER

♪♪ FRIENDLY'S SERE, UNHAPPY LOOK COULD have melted plastic.

It was on the tip of my tongue to say I'd suffered temporary amnesia from my attack, but the honest fact was that I'd really forgotten Snow in the mess that followed. I tried to fill Harve and Cop Boy in on the details. "She said she was attacked too! She said someone tried to stuff Elvis's favorite snack, a peanut-butter-and-banana sandwich, down her throat!"

"Oh, for God's sake in a hand basket," Friendly sputtered.

"Who?" Harve asked. "That girl out to the motel?"

"What did you do with her? Did you take her out to Ill Wind with you?"

"No, I didn't," I said defensively. "Listen, you have the night *I've* had and see if you can remember every little detail. Besides, you told me to stay away from the Lock and Load."

"So why didn't you?"

Well, I knew I was up against the wall on that one. How do you tell someone you went out there because the ghost of your ex-husband said it was a good idea? If I told them that, I wouldn't go to the detention center for obstructing justice, I'd been on my way to Clifton T. Perkins, the Maryland state hospital for the criminally insane. The one that was used as the model for Hannibal Lecter's jail in *The Silence of the Lambs*? Yeah, I could see myself up there, all right, doing a Thorazine shuffle and holding conversations with the walls.

So I did what I always do in situations like this: I changed the subject by describing the scene I had discovered at the Lock and Load. I edited Sam out, of course. But I wanted to get my version into the record, lest Vera and Albie's differ in any way.

"I got her calmed down and I dropped her off at the society editor's house for safekeeping," I explained. "Jolene owes me a favor, and I figured she'd be safe there." I decided not to mention the jeopardy to Jolene's precious Precious Moments.

"If, indeed, someone was attacking her," Friendly said skeptically. "Albie and the Widder Devine seem to think she entertained some pretty rough customers.''

''Well, that's the interesting thing. She said the person who attacked her looked like Elvis—just like the person who attacked me,'' I added as the pieces fell into place.

I waited for Friendly's usual string of colorful language, but he wasn't especially upset. Maybe it was taking a moment for him to collect his ideas too.

''Why didn't she call the police?'' Friendly asked finally.

''Because she's a hooker! We're the last people on the face of the earth she wants to deal with, Sarge,'' Harve pointed out.

Even Friendly had to see the logic of this. Nonetheless, I don't think it made him feel any better. He looked at his watch, then glanced at Vera and Albie, who were now studiously ignoring us and holding hands with the Elvii, raising their consciousness with a mantra.

''Harve, you stay here and keep an eye on those two,'' he commanded in an undertone. ''If they leave, radio a tail on them. Since you want to play Susie Detective, Hollis, you can come along to this Jolene's house so I can question Ms. White.''

''Right now? It's four o'clock in the morning! They're probably asleep!'' Fat chance, I thought to myself. ''Then she'll know I ratted her out!'' I added. ''I can't rat out a source.''

"She may be more than a source," Friendly said grimly. "You know, I can still charge you with obstructing and interfering. I could run your attractive behind down to the detention center right now. And I'm guessing Big Tuna ain't gonna get outta bed at this hour of the morning."

I bit my lower lip.

"Look," Harve said in a reasonable, we're-both-Eastern-Shore-people tone of voice, "Snow could be in a lot more trouble than she thinks she is. She may not have done anything in this case, but she could have seen or heard something that could hurt her. Maybe that's why she was attacked, didja think about that?"

"I guess you're right," I agreed. "I thought she was just gettin' hinky on me, but maybe you're right."

"We'll find out. Let's go."

IT WAS A QUIET RIDE IN THE FRIENDLYMOBILE TO Jolene's house. You could have cut the tension with a chain saw, it was that thick between us.

In the U.K., I understand, ratting out your sources is called assisting the police with their inquiries. On the Shore, it's called treason. Still, as little as I liked Snow's drug-induced life of prostitution and sleaze, I didn't want to see her harmed or killed. Or Jolene, for that matter, especially when I was having so much fun getting my own back on my least favorite coworker.

The lights were all on at Jolene's town house, upstairs and down. In the false dawn the storybook town houses seemed silent, shadowy, and threatening, like the Romanian village when there's a vampire epidemic.

The cold, when we got out of Friendly's Ranchero, was like a slap. It penetrated to the bone, cutting through layers of clothes like teeth.

I looked at the clouds my breath made in the air. They looked like thought balloons in a cartoon.

Friendly knocked gently on Jolene's door. "No sense embarrassing her in front of the neighbors. This isn't a raid," he whispered to me, and I looked guiltily at my feet, thinking about the very public way I'd trumpeted Snow's arrival.

Maybe, just maybe, Jolene didn't deserve that. Lack of sleep can awaken your conscience.

Nah, I decided, she deserved every second of it.

Friendly waited, then knocked again when there was no response. Then he tried the door.

The big grapevine wreath shuddered as the brightly painted door swung silently back on its hinges, revealing the wreckage in the living room.

It looked as if Martha Stewart had had a temper tantrum. Bits and pieces of grapevine wreath and shreds of pastel gingham were strewn across the once-white carpeting. The stuffing from a quilt floated in the air like giant dust motes. The sweet, intense smell of spilled peach potpourri oil was enough to gag a maggot. I watched in horror as Friendly's great big heel crunched down on the cherubic face of a porcelain figurine. Someone had done a good job of smashing all of those dead-baby angels into shards. It looked like they'd driven a truck through a Hallmark store. Wide-eyed dead-baby-angel face fragments glared at us from the rug.

"Holy shit," Friendly observed, pulling out his gun. "Stay behind me!"

We shuffled through the ruined dining area and into the kitchen, where it looked like that same someone had decided to make fruit soup, then changed their mind and just threw everything on the floor. And the walls. And the ceiling.

"Listen," Friendly said.

I listened.

There was a faint *thump-thump-thump* on the ceiling.

"Upstairs!" Friendly cried, and I followed him, really afraid of what we would find.

Unfortunately, I never got to see the rest of Jolene's country-cute decor. We found her lying on the landing in the upstairs hallway, bound and gagged with familiar red polyester scarves. They clashed with her pink lace bathrobe, but from the filthy look she shot me, I knew she was alive and sane. Only a fear-crazed Jolene would have been glad to see me.

Thank you, God, I added as Friendly undid her gag. "You—" she spit at me. "You did this to me! I hope you *die*!" There was something funny about seeing Jolene lying there, bound up like a Poultry Packer, and the first thing on her mind was my death.

"You might get your wish," I said, as Friendly took my Buck knife and cut her wrists and ankles free, thereby saving the knots as evidence, I noted with approval.

I expected Jolene to launch into a bout of hysterics, since that was her normal reaction to any stressful situation. But as she rubbed the circulation back into her wrists and ankles, she surprised me with her calm. "Some guy dressed up like Elvis came in. He tied me up and took off with Snow," she said in a voice that barely shook at all. Maybe she was just relieved to be rid of her. "She called him Zap. She knew him."

Cop Boy and I exchanged a look.

So it was Gadsen, and Snow knew him. He was our Elvis killer, I was certain of it.

And now he had Snow.

"How long ago?" Friendly asked.

Jolene, massaging her wrists, shrugged. "An hour, two hours? He just burst through the front door, which *she*"—Jolene tossed her head at me—"left unlocked when she dumped that . . . that drugged-out tramp off on me!"

"Dressed as Elvis?" Friendly was already punching in his cell phone.

"Yeah, the wig, the suit, the sunglasses—you know: Elvis. I'll press charges! Oh, you better believe I'll press charges after I finish suing Hollis and that slut! My Precious Moments that I spent years collecting are all gone!" Jolene being Jolene, she was more upset about this guy knocking over a few cheesy figurines than being an Elvis serial killer who could have easily done her in by cutting her throat with a broken CD or something.

"Can you recall anything about this man? Height? Weight? Age?" Friendly asked. Into the phone he was saying, "Yeah, I want an ambulance and an A.P.B. on a white? White male, possibly dressed in an Elvis outfit—yeah, an Elvis outfit! I know what I said! Just do it, Viola! He's traveling with a white female, approximately thirty-five, about five-eight, one-ten, blond hair. Possible kidnapping, assault, robbery, and B. and E. Possibly ID's as Zap Gadsen: G-a-d—dammit, Viola, don't get hinky on me now, I know he's *not* dead! No, not Elvis, Gadsen!" He remonstrated with the dispatcher. "No, Elvis is so dead! Gadsen's not—oh, just do what I tell you, and I'll explain later!"

"God, Jolene, I'm so sorry," I started to say. "I didn't know this was gonna happen. I'm so sorry he smashed up your stuff—"

I could hear the sirens growing closer. In a minute the place was going to be crawling with paramedics and cops.

Jolene gave me a look that peeled my paint. "He didn't do anything but tie me up, you idiot. *She* wrecked all my Precious Moments!"

I thought about that for a minute.

"I think Snow should get a medal," I murmured under my breath.

"And I think you ought to go home," Friendly said in a voice that was so quiet it scared me more than Jolene's rage. "You've done more than enough damage for a while. I'll get a uniform to drive you back to Dippy Donut so you can get your car."

So I went home in disgrace with fortune and cop's eyes.

16

I Can Help

♪ ♪ THE DAWN WAS BITTERLY COLD. THE THIN, angry wind had shifted down from the north, rattling through the bare branches of the winter trees.

As I let myself into my house, Venus, the Cat with an Attitude, whined and sailed in beneath my feet, tripping me up in her haste to hit the food dish. If I were her I wouldn't have been in such a hurry to come inside. It was colder in here than it was out, and that was saying something. The freezing wind rattled at the windows and whined for entrance.

"I was beginning to wonder if you were ever coming back. This place is as cold as hell's north gate, and believe me, I know how cold hell's north gate is."

"Where have you been while someone was trying to kill me?" I saw, without surprise, that Sam was sitting at the kitchen table. In the shadows he was barely visible, just a faint glow you could catch in the corner of your eye. It didn't take that long to fill him in, especially when he dismissed my near-death experience with a blithe almost-doesn't-count remark. No sympathy there. Nonetheless, I kept pouring out events until I'd exhausted the subject.

"I really messed it up good this time," I finished glumly.

"It can't be that bad," Sam offered in an Ann Landers, tell-me-all-about-it voice.

"I lost Snow White." As I dolloped out some Super Supper for Venus and set to work reviving the embers in the woodstove, I turned it all over one more time, shivering as I worked. Indeed, I probably told him more than he wanted to hear; I was in a mood for whining, and if a ghost and a half-feral cat were the only ones I could whine to, then they'd have to listen as I poured out my woes.

"So now it looks as if Zap Gadsen—who is not only alive but also an Elvis serial killer—has kidnapped Snow." I sighed as I piled on kindling, then a log, hovering by the open stove door as licks of flame slowly began to work their way up the sides of the wood. "And the thing is, I can't figure out the connections, but I know they're there. Albie can't or won't talk; Snow tried to talk and I wouldn't listen, and now she might be dead too."

After I'd warmed up my hands, I checked the taps in the kitchen sink. I'd opened them up a trickle so they wouldn't freeze but now I opened them all the way to defrost the tunnel of ice that had formed in the exposed joints of the pipes during the night. "Country living at its best," I said sourly, turning on the oven to add some heat to the house. "I hate it when it gets this cold, so that the edges of the house never feel quite warm and the drafts always seem to find me. But when you live on a reporter's salary in a cedar shake two-under-and-two-over former tenant house and pay rent to a landlord farmer who's tight as a tick, I guess you get what you pay for. Which in my case is thirty-two acres of rural privacy. I'd slit my own wrists before I'd live in some prechewed condo like Jolene or Friendly, where I could hear my neighbors through the walls," I grumbled to what I thought was a silent and sympathetic Sam.

Fortunately, I'd taken my shift as weekend reporter, so today—Sunday—was a day off for me. I could go to sleep now and sleep until seven tomorrow if I was so inclined, and I was so inclined.

"When in disgrace with fortune and cop's eyes, there's no such thing as too much sleep," I said.

I piled more logs into the woodstove and went wearily up the stairs to my bedroom. Without even showering I crawled under the quilts, where I found the book I had fallen asleep reading what seemed like a week ago. After a while Venus came up and joined me, snuggling against my legs for warmth.

The way I was feeling right then, she was better company than Friendly.

"I tried and failed on every level. Not only did I fail, but I placed Snow in harm's way," I said. Sam was sitting in his favorite seat, the old rocker by the window, impassively watching me rant and rave.

As I began to fall into an exhausted, depressed sleep, I sighed. "Snow is one tough cookie who knows how to take care of herself, right?" It sounded like cold comfort, even to me.

Sam merely rocked back and forth, watching me. I was too tired to fight with him or anyone else.

At least I hoped she was a tough cookie. "After all, the cops were on it, weren't they? How far could a guy dressed as Elvis get with a stoned-out, fighting hooker?"

Just as I was about to drift into a dead sleep, Sam said, "Oh, by the way, you got a couple of phone calls. Maybe you should check your voice mail."

His voice had that innocent tone I have come to mistrust. I opened one eye.

"It can wait until tomorrow," I muttered and closed that eye again, drifting off. "It's too cold to kill anybody."

"Did you remember to turn on the taps in the bathroom?" Sam asked. "You know how you hate it when the hot water in the shower freezes up.'' I heard the creak as the rocker swayed back and forth on the floorboards.

"Can't you do it?'' I asked.

"You know I can't waste my materializing talents on your plumbing,'' Sam reproved me.

Wearily, I stumbled out of bed and into the bathroom, where I opened up the hot-water tap to a trickle. Then I almost ran to get back into bed again; the floors were like slabs of ice.

"You know,'' Sam said, "while you're awake you really should check those messages.''

Cursing beneath my breath, I pick up the phone by the bed and punched in my Voice Mail codes. "One of these days,'' I hissed, "I'm calling an exorcist.''

"Hollis, this is Mom.''

I groaned.

"What's all this I hear about you bein' involved with one of Albie Lydekker's crazy schemes? Your cousin Jimmy Moe told your father down to the store that you were seen driving around town with that tramp Snow.'' A long, martyred sigh of the kind only a mother can produce. *"You know, honey, your father and I wish you would get married and have some babies and settle down like your brother, Robbie. Then you wouldn't have time to get into all this troub—''*

I punched the button that disconnected my mother's voice.

Sam had settled on the edge of the bed beside me, his ear against the handset as he leaned against me. He was cool and dry, like linen. I gave him a push, but my hand passed right through him.

"H-Hollis?"

Snow's voice gave me a heart jump.

"Are you there? Hollis, pick up, please! Hollis, Zap's got a hold of me and he wants to talk to you. He wants to negotiate."

The message ended as abruptly as it had started.

I looked at the phone as if it had turned into a snake and sunk its fangs into my hand. Then I looked at Sam, who had the grace to look only faintly smug.

"Now what?" I asked.

Sam grinned. "Check your Caller ID, of course. What's the use of this age of electronic miracles if you don't use 'em?"

I rushed down the stairs to the other phone on my desk. Shivering in the dim light, I punched the buttons and peered at the tiny screen on the little box.

Sam, who never bothered to walk when he could ride, appeared at my side in a puff of frosty mist. "Ah!" he said triumphantly. "There's your mother's number and, if I'm not mistaken, the number of the villain's hideout! Quick, Watson, call 'em back!"

"Is this long distance?" I asked.

"Oh, for God's sake, Holl! You never heard Sherlock Holmes bitching about a forty-five-cent phone call!" Sam sighed. I think he was ready to snatch the phone away from me and dial the number himself, except it was hard for him to make his fingers corporeal enough to push down on the buttons.

Nervously, I tapped out 4-1-0. "Oh, jeez, Sam, what if it *is* Albie? I'll kill him!"

"Just punch it out," Sam commanded, "and stay calm."

My fingers were shaking as I squeezed out those last seven digits. "I've never even heard of this exchange," I said. "Where is it?"

"Probably a cell phone," Sam suggested tightly. He placed his head beside mine, listening as the clicks and buzzes on the phone connected, and it began to ring.

And ring, and ring.

"I guess nobody's home," I giggled nervously. Nervously? I was scared to death.

The phone rang again. It sounded long and hollow at the other end of the line, as if it were ringing in an empty room. Then someone picked up.

"Hello?" A man's voice.

For a moment I couldn't respond; he sounded so . . . so calm, like I'd just gotten him up from a nap or something. Then I realized that he was using one of those electronic things to alter his voice. Her voice?

"Uh, this is, uh, Hollis Ball?"

"Oh, yes, how kind of you to return Ms. White's call," the voice at the other end said genially. Then I realized he/she/it was doing a damned good electronic Elvis impression. Chills ran up and down my spine.

I looked at Sam, and he looked at me. We were both puzzled. Surely, he should have sounded like Professor Moriarity, at the very least? Elvis was not the voice I expected from a deep-dish bad guy. Sam gestured for me to continue.

"Uh, so, uh, is Snow okay?" I asked while Sam nodded approvingly.

"She's as well as can be expected. Between you and me"—the man lowered his voice confidentially—"I really think she has a leee-tle drug and alcohol problem."

"That's the understatement of the year," I gasped.

"In more ways than one," Sam offered.

"Shhh!" I told my ex, forgetting.

"Is there someone there with you?" the voice asked with a hint of concern.

"No," I said quickly. "I was talking to my cat." Sam made a face.

"Ah. So, what can I do for you?" the voice asked.

Well, I guess he had a point. I had called *him.*

I sucked in a deep breath and forced myself to sound calm. "Well, you could give me back Snow," I suggested.

"Yes, I suppose I could." He sighed. "But that wouldn't really help me much, would it?"

"She's okay, isn't she?"

"As well as can be expected under the circumstances. I gave her some of my Quaaludes, and that seemed to calm her down, at least enough to sleep. I really dislike these creative types; they're so self-centered.''

''You can say that again,'' I agreed. ''So, look''—I reached for a notebook and a pen—''why did you take her away in the first place?''

''Because she knows too much, of course. But she doesn't know what she knows, alas. It's almost all over for me, anyway. I've pretty well botched everything,'' he said regretfully.

''I so do love a civilized villain,'' Sam muttered. ''Where in hell is he?''

''Are you really Zap Gadsen?'' I asked. ''Didn't you drown?''

''Oh, I can't tell you all that on the phone. There might be a tap on your wire,'' he said fretfully.

''I don't think so. All I've got is Caller ID and voice mail. I think the tap costs extra, and my phone bills are already too high.''

''Tell me about it.'' He sighed. ''It costs a fortune just to do business these days. E-mail is cheaper, you know.''

I scrabbled in my numb brain for something to say. In the background on the other end, I could hear a slow, rhythmic clanking sound. It was vaguely familiar, but I couldn't place it, perhaps because I wanted to so very badly. ''Keep talking,'' Sam hissed. ''Keep him on the phone.''

"I know, I know," I said to the voice in what I hoped sounded like a sympathetic tone. "So tell me, what do I have to do to get Snow back?"

There was laughter. "Come to the Elvis contest. I'll see you there. And I'll tell you then what I want in exchange for Ms. White's life. You can see that I haven't decided to kill her—yet. Nor will I, if you do as I say."

"But how will I know you?" I asked the caller while swatting ineffectually at Sam.

He laughed. "Oh, you'll know me," he promised. "And by the way, not a word to your police friends, please. You see, I do know a great deal about you."

"By the way, that was you who tried to run me over with that Caddy, then strangle me, wasn't it?"

"I am sorry about that. But what choice did I have?"

"Well, you didn't have to try to kill me. That was really rude."

"My abject apologies, but situated as I am, don't expect me to send a bouquet to express my regrets, much as I would like to. Good morning, Ms. Ball. So nice to talk to you."

I listened to the dial tone buzzing in my ear.

"Damn," Sam whispered. "The Elvis contest. That's tonight! Elvis's birthday!"

"My, how the time flies when you're having fun," I observed dryly. "Sam, what are we gonna *do*?"

"With your puny mortal hearing, you evidently

missed a most important clue," my ghostly ex-husband replied loftily. "But I, with my superbly acute ghost sense, was able to discern it, even with a lousy connection."

"Oh, stop talking like a Marvel Comic," I snapped. "I heard some sort of clanging, like a bell. I've heard it before, but I can't remember where!" I started pacing out my frustration, walking up and down the kitchen floor. Venus, sensing the possibility of food, appeared and began to rub seductively against Sam's translucent leg, purring happily. She has no taste in men, but then, maybe she gets that from me.

Sam bent and scratched behind Venus's ears. She responded by going into an ecstatic stretch. "Think, think, think, think," Sam muttered to himself. All he needed was a deerstalker hat and a meerschaum pipe. And, of course, a shot of seven percent solution.

"A bell, but not like a church bell or anything," I ruminated, hopping from one cold foot to the other. It was a wonder I didn't get frostbite. "D'you suppose it really was Gadsen, Sam? Is he alive and out there somewhere killing people?"

"Could be him, could be Vera, could even be Albie," Sam suggested. "You've got to be prepared for the fact that it could be Albie."

"I don't understand any of this. What's the connection, aside from the gambling?" I shivered.

"D'you think whoever this is is just killing people because he likes killing people?"

"Well, he could have killed your pal Snow at any time; there's no one more vulnerable than a prostitute." Sam narrowed his eyes. "Remember when someone was killing all those crack whores in Bethel? How the killer would strangle them and dump their bodies in the Santimoke, and they would drift over to Beddoe's Island?"

"And one washed up next to Toby's boat and someone said, 'Damn, Toby, you're hard on your dates?' "

We looked at each other. "The Mandrake Shoal buoy!" we both said at once.

"I'd know that mournful clang anywhere," Sam exclaimed. "Remember how we used to sail out there on hot summer nights, drop anchor, and just lie around in the cockpit, drinking Heinies and looking at the stars?"

"Yeah, I do," I replied. The Mandrake Shoal buoy, that big old orange channel marker out there at the mouth of the creek, where it flows into the Santimoke. Near Rolley Shallcross's house. "What does this mean, Sam?"

He grinned triumphantly. "It means that your girl is being held prisoner near the marker!"

"On a boat!" I yelled, jumping up and down. "There was a boat moored off the dock at Ill Wind, which isn't that far from Mandrake Shoal—"

"Yes!" Sam crowed, and we high-fived each other. Of course, my hand went right through his, but it didn't matter.

Venus, startled, gave a yowl and hid under the kitchen table, where she growled at us imperiously.

"Quick, Watson! The game is afoot!" Sam exclaimed.

17

TRYIN' TO GET TO YOU

♪♪ WHEN MY TIME COMES, I WOULD LIKE MY epitaph to read, *Out of Print*. I am afraid that what it *will* end up saying is, *Well, it seemed like a good idea at the time.*

Unfortunately, by the time Sam and I put our foolproof plan and our airtight alibi into action, it didn't seem quite as, well, cool as it did when we were hatching it.

In fact, it was downright freezing.

You try paddling a canoe in subzero weather across open water. "I wonder how the Eskimos do it," I muttered through chattering teeth and my bulky orange survival suit.

"Now I bet you're glad you bought this thing," Sam said from the bow, where he was perched, weightless on the inflated plastic, like a ghostly fig-urehead. Of course, you couldn't expect him—being a spirit—to paddle, but at least a canoe has the advan-tage of being low in the water and silent in movement. "You saw the C-Mart ad in the paper and you said, 'Oh, I won't use that thing,' and I said, 'Trust me. For a reporter, a flotation device—even an inflatable ca-noe—will come in handy,' and it has, hasn't it?"

I grunted, which he could read any damned way he chose; he wasn't paddling it up a certain proverbial creek on a search-and-rescue mission after a murderer and a grunge queen.

At least the boat was out there. If it hadn't been there, I don't know what we would have done.

Beneath the dark cover of a cloudy dawn, we moved silently through the gray water toward the big cabin cruiser moored just off Mandrake Shoal. The only sound was the mournful toll of the electronic bell and the small tinkle of my paddle as we moved through a steady chop of incoming tide. Not even the watermen were abroad.

Since we'd set out from the public landing about a quarter of a mile downcreek, the cold had become increasingly cold and sharp over the water until it felt as if it was biting into my cheeks and fingers. Fortu-nately, the wind had shifted northwest and steady, or I could have been in serious trouble. I like canoeing, but I prefer shallow water in warm weather; I'm no-body's guts-and-glory girl, and I didn't intend to die a heroine. Or so I told my self as the cabin cruiser grew closer and closer.

She was a good-size boat, one of those flashy Grand Banks fiberglass jobs, about as wide as they are long. A fishing boat for old Viagra guys with gold chains, cruising up and down the Bay's hot spots with babes in bikinis posing on the prow. I was willing to bet no one had ever baited as much as a hook on this Ego Alley special.

"It has to be Gadsen's boat; no one else would be out here in a boat like that in the middle of winter," I muttered.

As she bobbed at its mooring, she looked large and foreboding, like a big old hunk of floating evil. I saw no running lights and mentally added that to the killer's list of transgressions.

"Oh, yeah, Your Honor, three counts of first-degree homicide and one of operating a vessel without running lights," I whispered, warming myself by picturing Frank Carroll throwing the book at the killer for mooring without navigation signals.

"It's too quiet," Sam observed uneasily.

"Can you, like, discorporate here and go aboard and check things out?" I asked.

Sam tsked. "You know ghosts can't cross running water," he said primly.

"This is a great time to tell me!" I hissed angrily. "Now what?"

"Why are you asking me? I thought you had the

plan.'' Sam turned to me, the picture of outraged dead white European maleness.

The boat was no more than a few yards away; I could read the name on her stern board:

Hound Dog
Watertown, MD

"Figures," I grumbled, circling the boat. From where I was sitting, down on the water alongside her chine, her sheer looked like the Alps. "Sam, this is a *biiiig* boat," I whispered dubiously.

"There's a diving platform on the stern." Sam beckoned to me. "Tie up there and we'll climb on board, like the pirates do."

"I-rate pi-rates," I muttered, wondering how Sam knew so much about stealth boarding. All those living years when he had deserted me to disappear in the Caribbean were still a big blank space. But I was afraid the closest he'd ever gotten to Caribbean pirates was the ride at Disney World.

Nonetheless, I cautiously paddled the canoe around to *Hound Dog*'s stern. There was, indeed, a wooden diving platform affixed to her so that happy swimmers could climb over the stern-board ladder and ease themselves in and out of the water.

I tied the painter to a strut and unsteadily shifted one foot from the canoe to the platform, grasping for the ladder as I did so. My .38, tucked in the chest pocket of my suit, pressed against my stomach; I could feel the cold metal through several layers of thermals and was oddly comforted. Like a good patriotic American, I was armed and dangerous.

Sam floated easily above my head, perching on the stern board, invisible, as he scouted out the lay of the craft. "All clear on deck," he said, and I waited for a swell to pull myself up on the ladder, swaying for a moment over that frigid gray water before I found my balance. Looking down, I could see the translucent sheets of ice forming on the surface of the creek. I shivered.

"Careful," Sam said. "Last thing you want to do is go overboard."

Well, I knew that, but I was too anxious to say anything as I climbed up to peer over the stern board into an empty deck.

"Go see where he is," I instructed Sam. "See if you can find Snow down there someplace."

"Okay," he said and disappeared into a misty puff of frost.

It was quiet; the only sound was the splash and slap of water in the bilge and the mournful heartbeat of the electronic bell, warning the unwary that the creek was hazardous.

I hung on that ladder for what seemed like hours as the boat rose and fell and the water slapped around in the bilge. Slowly, it began to occur to me that this boat was much *too* quiet. Somewhere, a bilge pump should be starting and stopping; a generator should have whirred to life from time to time; the refrigerator in the galley should be making some kind of hum. I stared at the empty fiberglass box of the cockpit, at the teak wheel and the chrome gearbox, the eleventy-seven toys mounted on the rising beam: Loran, Fish Finder, Bimbo Alert, radios, radar—all those toys men can't live without. And none of it was working. Her power was shut down completely. *Hound Dog* was dead, but not dead, something worse. It was as if she was holding her breath, waiting for something. Something like the next victim.

Oh, my God, I thought, I'm aboard a floating Hill House, the Overlook Hotel of boats.

And still Sam didn't come back.

Thin dawn began to seep across the creek, a water-color-pink stain just brushing the tops of the pines on the east shore. It might have been pretty if I weren't so cold and tired and scared.

And still Sam didn't come back.

I think it was at that point that it began to sink in just how nuts this venture was. Unfortunately, it was sort of too late to do anything about it.

Finally, when I could feel my own sweat trickling down my back through my thermal underwear, I took a deep breath and crawled up on the stern, ready to jump down and paddle away at the first sign of trouble.

The cabin door was closed, the glass opaque with

frost. Heart beating, I crossed what felt like the longest expanse of open and exposed deck in the world and tried the latch on the door.

It swung open on oiled hinges. I squinted into the gloom. The only light came from the portholes, but I discerned the chromium gleam of a galley and head to starboard and what appeared to be a hatch table and banquette seats to port. A fairly typical nautical layout. Beyond that there was a set of louvered doors, but they were closed. A ladder went up to the bridge, where there would be a second helm for foul weather, but the hatchway was closed and hooked. A third ladder descended into the engine room and the hull.

"I'll take curtain three, Monty," I muttered, heading straight ahead.

The louvers swung back. I peered into a narrow passageway without light. A closed door to the left, a closed door to the right, and a closed door straight ahead. Sleeping quarters, I thought. The stateroom must be dead ahead.

I thrust my hand into the chest pocket of my overalls and pulled out my gun, cocking the trigger the way Friendly had taught me. Holding the barrel with both hands, finger on the trigger, I flattened myself against the starboard wall and cautiously moved ahead.

In spite of the cold, sweat froze on my forehead and clung to my back. I took a deep breath, wondering where the hell Sam was.

I inched toward the stateroom door at the end of the passage, keeping my eyes on the latch. If it turned I would go into a firing stance. Claustrophobia, never far away with me, singed the borders of my concentration.

And then, the cabin door slammed shut, leaving me in darkness.

"Hey," Sam said casually.

In the darkness I could see just the luminous outline of his form. I had to take a couple of deep breaths before my heart could slow down.

"I found her; she's in the master cabin forward," he said. "But I didn't see anyone else."

"Is she okay?"

I sensed rather than saw Sam screw up his face. "About as okay as you'd expect," he said. "She's zonked out."

We found Snow sprawled across the bed in the forward cabin. She was wrapped in blankets and snoring so loudly it was a wonder we hadn't heard her back at the landing.

I shook her shoulder. "Snow? Snow?" I asked, sitting down on the bed.

She opened one eye. "Znoook," she groaned, closing it again and rolling over.

She didn't look fabulous, but then again, I hadn't expected her to. There were deep purple circles under her eyes, and she was wearing a flannel Kountry Kutie nightgown, obviously borrowed from Jolene, but at least she was alive.

"Snow, what happened?" I persisted, shaking her.

"Got any drugs?" she asked. A thin string of saliva dribbled along the side of her lip and across the bed. She kept her eyes closed. "Man, who turned the lights on?" she demanded irritably. "Man dressed up like Elvis. Gave me some niiiiice downers. Lemme sleep, man." Then she zoned out again.

Snow coughed, rolled over, and began to snore again, a sound like thousands of tiny saw blades running across a chalkboard. She looked as happy as a pig in poop, and why shouldn't she?

"Now what?" I asked Sam.

He shrugged. "I thought you might have an idea, huh? I mean, *you* were the one who wanted to rescue her."

"I want a cigarette," I whined. "When we get back to land, I'm buying a pack of cigarettes and I'm chain-smoking every last one of them as fast as I can!"

"Those things can kill you," someone said.

I froze, then slowly twisted around.

Elvis was standing there. No, it wasn't Elvis, it was someone wearing the drag. The blue-black pompadour wig, the silver shades, the Vegas jumpsuit.

And he was holding a gun.

I reached for mine; I'd dropped it on the bed when I'd gone to Snow's aid.

"Ah, ah, ah!" Elvis said, waving the gun from side to side at me. He talked like him too, that poured-molasses southern drawl. "Put your hands up, please. Thank you, thank you very much."

"This is an interesting twist," Sam remarked conversationally.

"I thought you said you checked the whole boat," I said to him, raising my hands.

"I did!" Sam replied.

"I didn't say anything," Elvis told me.

"I was talking to my ghost," I replied. Well, when someone's pointing a gun at me, I'm clearly not at my best.

"That's very funny," Elvis replied in a tone that indicated it wasn't. "Now, get up. Slowly."

I did as I was told, rising from the bed on shaky legs.

"Let's go up on the deck," Elvis commanded. "You first, Ms. Ball."

Again, I did as I was told.

It was full morning light now, and the shock of the cold air made me gasp as I opened the door to the deck.

"How did you find me?" Elvis asked curiously, as if having a normal social conversation were the most natural thing in the world. I had to hand it to this person; he was one cool customer. He *had* to be Zap Gadsen. Who else but a lawyer would be so bloodless?

I looked at the barrel of the gun, still pointed at me. It was nickel-plated. It gleamed brightly in the sunlight. It's funny, the things you notice when you're in mortal danger. It might be the last thing I notice, I thought. Sam was nowhere to be seen.

"We—I heard the sound of the shoal marker when I called you. I figured it out from there." Now I could see Ill Wind, Elvis Man's house, right across the water, not five hundred yards away from shore. No doubt there were plenty of cops over there, but none of them would think to look out across the creek. Why should they?

"We?" Elvis shook his head. "Who's we?"

"Why, my ghost and I," I replied.

"Oh, right. I forgot." He smiled and shook his wig. "You're funny, Ms. Ball. Very funny. As funny as a turd in a punch bowl." This last was snarled.

"And you're Zap Gadsen, right?"

"No, I'm Elvis," he replied seriously, and then I knew I was dealing with someone who was a slice of cheese short of a reality burger. "I used to be Zap Gadsen though, before I became Elvis."

"Okay," I agreed. "Who am I to argue?"

"Nobody," he told me seriously. "Because you're going to be dead, okay?"

"Oh." Well, that left me nonplussed for a minute.

"You won't feel a thing," he promised. "Because you're going to fall overboard and be found drifting along with that silly raft of yours. I understand hypothermia is quick and painless.''

''Yeah, but suppose I don't want to fall overboard?'' I asked.

''Well, then I'll have to shoot you, and you can die a long and painful death. Then I can throw you overboard,'' he concluded triumphantly. ''I wish you weren't so hard to kill,'' he added, as if that were my fault too.

I thought about that for a moment. It was hard to take a death threat seriously from someone dressed as Elvis. Besides, I was sure that Sam would come to my rescue. At least I sure hoped he would.

''So why didn't you kill Snow?'' I wondered.

''Because she will be my Priscilla when I claim my rightful place as the King incarnate. And I'll have to get rid of you because you were trying to take her away from me. You took her to that woman's house, the place with allo' them figurines. I knew, because I followed you. You shouldna done that, Ms. Ball. It wasn't right.''

And people thought Rolley Shallcross was a wack job! I suppose I should have known from the name Zap and all the pills he was taking that he was crazy, but sometimes I'm a little slow on the uptake. Fortunately, as a small-town reporter, I've had plenty of practice dealing with the sanity-challenged.

''It's really sad that you had to track us down,'' Gadsen/Elvis said mournfully. ''I really hate to have to kill someone. It used to be that I just shot out TV's. I never knew that assuming the mantle of the King would be so difficult,'' he fretted.

"But why did you kill Bang Bang? And Elvis Man? Where did you come from after all this time?''

Zap/Elvis pursed his lips. ''I didn't kill Bang Bang,'' he said, confused. ''He was gonna help me realize my dream of an Elvis casino, right here in Watertown. I *had* to kill Rolley. I'd been hiding out with him since I faked the drowning, and he knew too much, so he had to die.''

"And you tried to kill Snow by shoving a peanut-butter-and-banana sandwich down her throat.''

The gun wavered, but not enough. ''Bang's dead?'' All those downers made him a bit slow-witted. He looked downright upset. His lower lip quivered. ''Somebody killed Bang? But why?''

"I wish I knew.'' This was getting old; I was beginning to wish he'd kill me and get it over with. ''Look, you don't *really* want to kill me, do you?''

"Of course I do,'' he admitted. ''Oh, I can't believe Bang's dead! He was my best friend! He said when he got everything straightened out, I'd have my Elvis casino, right there in Watertown on the waterfront. And I could be Elvis every night!'' He was so distraught, I almost felt sorry for him. Tears rolled down his checks behind his big old Elvis glasses, and his lip trembled. ''He can't be d-dead!''

"But he is,'' said a voice behind us, and we both

turned to look at Snow as she emerged from the forward cabin. The sharp morning light was not really flattering to her; you could see the way a hard life had treated her looks.

But that sharp morning light sure did glint off the black barrel of the gun she had trained on us.

Like I say, you have to love America; everyone's armed and dangerous. And I especially had to appreciate it because she had my trusty .38, which should have been lying on the bed in the stateroom next to her unconscious self.

Zap didn't seem to be appreciating an American's God-given right to bear arms at that moment; he turned, pulled the trigger, and the hammer snapped down on a shot so loud that my ears hurt. "Good-bye, honey," he said.

The bullet drove itself into the rising beam inches above Snow's head.

"You always were a wuss," Snow replied.

And then she fired.

I gave a choked half scream as a big hole appeared in Zap's head, right below his wig. Slowly, he crumbled to the deck in a puddle of dead spangles.

"What did you go and do that for?" I asked peevishly. "I had the whole thing under control. Besides, he didn't kill Bang."

"No, of course he didn't," Snow said, smiling. "I did."

18

IT'S NOW OR NEVER

♪♪ "ALL OF A SUDDEN," I SAID THICKLY, "I'M remembering why I didn't like you in high school. You were a sneaky bitch who'd steal a boyfriend or loot a gym locker without a second thought. In fact, hadn't there been some trouble about the missing yearbook money?"

"You are so lame." Snow sighed. "Now, I expect you'll want me to tell you why I killed Bang Bang?" Even though she looked ridiculous in that pastel flannel nightgown, I wasn't about to take my eye off her. I mean, suppose she wanted to kill me next? And where the hell was Sam?

"Well, that would help," I said. "I always like to know what's happening."

"That's because you were always nosy. No wonder

you became a reporter. It's a way to get paid for gossiping!''

Well, she had me there. I could have made some crack about why she became a slut, but with crazy Zap Gadsen lying dead on the deck, I figured discretion was the better part of staying alive.

But I'd forgotten one other thing about Snow: She couldn't keep her mouth shut. If she stole your boyfriend or your pocketbook, the whole school would find out about it sooner or later, because she would tell all her hitter girlfriends about it while they grabbed a smoke in the downstairs girls' bathroom while cutting classes.

''I used to work for Bang in Baltimore, in his club on the Block. Before there was a Vera, I was his main old lady. When it looked like the state would legalize casinos sooner or later, he was the first to see the potential of the Eastern Shore. Bang thought, the tourists already came here, so why not stop and gamble? He gave Zap Gadsen a lot of money to buy up those old canneries down on the waterfront in Watertown. See, it was Bang Bang's idea to set up a paper corporation, so no one would know that he was involved. He needed to launder some money from his other businesses. Bang had a rap sheet, you know.''

''Yeah, I guess I could figure that.'' It was freezing out there; I wondered how she could stand there in nothing but a flannel nightgown and her bare feet. But

Snow *was* a tough cookie; she was enjoying this too much to feel the cold.

"So, like I said, Bang set up a dummy corporation to buy up real estate. That was B and B Enterprises. And Zap was supposed to quietly go around and buy up all those old wrecked buildings."

"Supposed to?"

"Yeah." Snow smiled, and it was not a nice smile. "Well, whattya know? Zap takes the money and disappears. Allegedly falls off the boat, right?"

"So far I follow you."

"Well, Bang figures the money's gone along with Zap. Which is a big loss, but about then Bang Bang's old man died. Crabby Devine left him another pile of money, so Bang's back in the game. He gets me to buy up the property cheap as B and B Enterprises. He was supposed to cut me in. But he didn't, the pig. He dumped me and went off and *married* that Elvis hippie freak, after everything I did for him." Snow's tone was bitter. I could identify with that, having been a woman scorned myself.

"So you offered Bang Bang in revenge?"

"I coulda done it a lot better if that asshole Albie hadn't been around. It was easy to whack him; I just waited till he was zonked on his damned pills, then I went into the bathroom and got him from the side with one of those stupid scarves. I enjoyed watching the son of a bitch die." She smiled.

"That was the last blow job I thought I'd ever have

to give. Do you have any idea what it's like to do a guy in an Elvis suit?"

"As a matter of fact—"

But it was Snow's story, and she wasn't interested in *my* kinky Elvis experience. She never was a good listener.

"See, when Bang got married and threw me out and I set up shop at the Lock and Load, I got to know poor Rolley. Elvis Man might not have been the brightest bulb on the string, but he was sweet and he treated me with respect. I really liked Rolley, you know," she said wistfully, pushing an errant strand of lank hair out of her face. "He was like a little kid. He trusted everybody. Including that pig."

She nodded toward Gadsen, who was oozing blood across the deck.

"Bang and Zap and Rolley all knew each other from the Elvis circuit; they were all collectors. Bang'd set up Rolley as the manager of the Lock and Load when B and B bought it, as a joke, more or less. When Zap staged his accident, he moved in with Rolley. It was easy to get Rolley to hide him out while Zap tried to figure out how to reappear and get his hands on that old waterfront cannery. All that property was still in Rolley's name."

She lifted her head, looking sideways at me. "Sometimes all a john wants to do is talk. You know, they just need someone to listen. And Rolley told me that Zap was back. Zap was so crazy about Elvis, so crazy, he really thought he was Elvis. They called him Elvis over in Annapolis, and it made him so happy, poor son of a bitch. Anyway, when I came back it was Rolley who let me in on his big secret. Zap wasn't dead; he'd taken Bang Bang's money and disappeared. See, he was about to get disbarred for some other shaky shit he'd been up to. But Zap was hiding out at Ill Wind, Rolley's place. What an idiot! All that Elvis crap would have driven me as crazy as it did those three. But Zap thought he was clever and that no one would ever find him there. But I did. Like I said, Rolley didn't have a lot of friends, but he had me, and he told me everything. When Zap thought Rolley had ratted him out to Bang, he killed him. And I killed Bang for what he did to me. And now I've killed Zap for Rolley. Rolley would have wanted it that way."

"And then there were none," I said.

"And then there was me. And the real estate."

"How do you figure into that?" I asked.

Snow laughed. "Rolley invested all his money in Elvis collectibles! You look in that house, you're lookin' at a million dollars' worth of Elvis stuff! Old records, glasses—hell, I'll bet he's got Elvis's underwear in there! All invested in Elvis. Why, he's even bought up a pair of Elvis's blue suede shoes!" She laughed bitterly. "Perfect, innit? Talk about a way to launder money!"

"Perfect," I agreed.

"Stuff Elvis touched goes up and up and up in value. People pay big money for his old Q-tips or whatever. There's even a couple of Elvis's old cars in the garage! It's appreciated so much over the years that a lot of it is worth three times what Rolley paid for it! It's better than a mutual fund! The three of them loved Elvis. Me, I can take him or leave him, but I shoulda known better. Because when Bang ran into a bitch who told him she could channel the King, I got sent back to the Shore 'to keep an eye on things,' he says, the lying bastard. What he meant was he wanted a clear field with his New Age chickie-poo, and me outta the way. I'm cut off, I'm nobody. I got to live in a roach motel, she's in the big house in Roland Park and sunnin' her creepy behind on this boat in the islands all winter while I'm freezing with no heat at the Lock and Load! Next thing you know I'm turning tricks; Bang cut off the money. Oh, Bang was a real sweetheart."

A biting gust of wind rippled her thin flannel nightgown, but she never even flinched.

"But I wasn't as much of a druggie as everyone thought I was," Snow continued. "As long as every-one thought I was a stoned-out hooker, I could keep a lookout for myself. See, *I* was the silent partner in B and B. And Bang thought I was too zonked to know or care what was going on. He figured I'd be dead with a spike in my arm in six months. The rotten prick." Her mouth curled, and she spewed out her rage with all the passion of a woman used and abused. "I spiked him first, the prick."

"But what about Zap?" I asked.

Snow shrugged. "As soon as Rolley cued me in that Zap was alive and hiding out at his house"—she jerked her head in the direction of Ill Wind, across the creek—"well, I called Bang Bang right away. I had my plan. You wouldn't believe how fast he came over here to whack Zap. See, Bang was planning on setting up Albie for the murder, because Bang found out his love-and-peace hippie wife was doin' the New Age nasty with Albie. So Bang had to create this whole Elvis contest as an excuse for Albie to be over here in the first place. Bang always thought he was so smart. But I was smarter. I got him before he could get Albie set up."

"So Albie and Vera were a thing all along?" I demanded angrily. "You mean Albie wouldn't have been involved in this mess in the first place if he'd kept his pants on?"

Snow nodded. "Too bad for Albie. Too bad for Zap too. He would have killed you to protect me. He really thought I was his Priscilla."

"Talk about your hard-boiled dames," I said admiringly. "But who tried to kill you at the Lock and Load with a peanut-butter-and-banana sandwich?"

"Nobody, stupid. I made it all up when I saw you snooping around back last night. I figured you might be getting too close to the truth, and that was Zap pounding on the door, by the way. How was I to know you were gonna try to rescue me? You were so cute, trying to rescue me. Jesus, why did you have to take me to that woman's house? I almost had to kill *her*, she was so annoying.

"I was never so glad to be busted out in my life as when Zap found me there. I thought you'd take me to your house, see. Then I could have done you in at my leisure."

"Oh, what the pluperfect hell! No good deed goes unpunished," I grumbled. And speaking of pluperfect hell, where was Sam?

"You know too much. You were starting to track the paper trail of B and B Enterprises. It would have led you right to me. According to the terms of the incorporation, see, the last living partner gets everything. And I intend to own that property. There's an election coming up, and both of the front-runners in the governor's race endorse casino gambling in Maryland. Maybe not this year, and maybe not next, but when some gambling company wants a location in Santimoke County, I'll be sitting on some great waterfront property."

"Boy, you are one smart girl, Snow," I said. "I'll be damned."

"You probably will be," she agreed, advancing on me. "I'll give you the same choice Zap gave you."

"Fast death by hypothermia or slow death by bullet?" I asked. "Gee, let me think!"

Where the hell was Sam?

I backed away from Snow, keeping my eye on the gun. I just hated the idea of being shot with my own firearm. It was such a cliché. If I'm going to die, I decided, I am gonna take you down with me. I guess at that point I'd had enough of other people's problems.

I moved forward and she shot. I felt the bullet whiz past my head.

Well, I could have told her it fired a little to the left, but she never asked. But the recoil made her take a step back, and as she did, her bare feet slipped on the icy deck and she went into a skid.

I rolled, but not fast enough; she skimmed across me and tripped over Zap's body. It sent her over the gunnel, flying. The last I saw, she was all bare feet and flannel hurtling over the side.

I heard the splash as she hit the creek.

I looked down into the water and saw her struggling, treading water. The look she gave me was pure loathing.

"Try to make it around to the diving platform," I commanded her, heading for the stern. I made it down the ladder, my boots feeling heavy and awkward, and clung to one of the struts as I knelt on the icy boards and stretched out a hand toward her.

"I-I can't swim!" she yelled, thrashing around.

"You don't have to! Just calm down and try to

float toward me. Keep moving! Keep moving!" I shouted frantically. "Keep moving toward me!"

Slowly, she began to work her arms and legs, struggling to keep her head above the icy water. Inch by inch she fought the current, moving around the hull of the boat toward me. Her blond hair was plastered to her skull; I could hear her teeth chattering above the sound of her flailing.

Gripping the strut with one hand, I leaned out toward the tethered canoe, reaching for the paddle. If I could grasp it, I could offer it to her and pull her to the platform. If I could get her to the platform, I could get her out of the water.

But maddeningly, the inflatable canoe bobbed just out of reach. With only one free hand, I couldn't pull the line toward me fast enough; each time I got a handful of plastic rope, it would slide out of my numbing fingers again. The red and yellow boat with its blue paddle bobbed just out of my reach.

I dared not loosen my grip on the strut: I knew if I went overboard, my rubber boots would fill up with water, weighing me down to the bottom of the creek.

"Keep moving, keep moving!" I shouted, oblivious to the irony of trying to save a woman who had just tried to kill me. In an emergency we do what we've been trained to do without thinking about the moral issues. Her hand reached out, and our fingers brushed. Just as I leaned to grab her wrist, a wave washed her away from me.

Snow struggled, but the incoming tide was too strong; she was caught on the current, and it was pulling her away from the boat.

With just that thin nightgown, she had no defense against the numbing cold of the water.

The last thing I saw of her were her eyes, boring into mine as she slowly stopped struggling to keep her head above water.

I knew the moment that she decided to let the cold take her; I saw the resignation in her eyes as she sank beneath the gray waves.

Far away I heard the slow, steady clang of the Mandrake Shoal bell.

And then I heard the sirens of the Marine Police Whalers.

I tried to stand up, but my legs were shaking so bad, they couldn't hold me. I watched as the tongues of icy water lapped at the knees of my survival suit and waited for someone else to make decisions.

I'd made enough for one day. I closed my eyes.

"Hey." I heard a voice above my head and looked up.

Sam, ghostly Sam, golden in the morning light, looked down at me. "What did I miss?" he asked.

19

GOOD ROCKIN' TONIGHT

♪ ♪ OH, I FORGOT. I GUESS YOU WANT TO KNOW about the Elvis contest, having read all this way.

Albie and Vera did manage to salvage it. They really worked to fix up the old cocktail lounge at the Lock and Load, or at least, the two of them managed to paint the place and get a stage set up by January 16, which, as you know, is Elvis's birthday.

And a good thing too, because they sold a lot of tickets, and a lot of people came out.

I guess Vera and Albie are really a thing; at least she seems to be able to keep him from the worst of his gambling excesses. We'll see. With Albie, you just never know.

But he didn't even give odds on the contestants. Which was a good thing too, as it turned out.

And all the Elvii who weren't dead gave a great performance. Shelvis, Drac-Elvis, and Waterman Elvis did a lot better than you might think.

Frank and Friendly and I agreed that we had no idea there was this much Elvis talent on the Eastern Shore, and we thought it was really going to be hard to pick just one first-prize winner.

But there was this one guy who was really terrific. I mean, he really *was* Elvis. You'd have sworn that it was the King up there in his pink and black suit, singing ''Viva Las Vegas!''

The thing is, when Vera went to give him his first-prize award, he wasn't anywhere to be found, and when she checked, he wasn't on the roster either. Nobody knew him, no one saw him come in, and no one saw him leave. It was the strangest thing, and that's what I told Sam later too.

My ghost just laughed. ''Didn't you check out his feet?'' he asked.

I guess E can rest easy now.

He's got his blue suede shoes back.